After the Apocalypse - A Story of Pandemic Survival

Book One—The Old Man

Chris Russell

Trenton, Georgia

Print ISBN: 978-0-9772342-0-2
Ebook ISBN: 978-0-9772342-1-9

Published by BookLocker.com, Inc., Trenton, Georgia.

BookLocker.com, Inc.
2025

First Edition

Library of Congress Cataloging in Publication Data
Russell, Chris
After the Apocalypse - A Story of Pandemic Survival
by Chris Russell
Library of Congress Control Number: 2024926576

Dedications

It takes a village...that's too cliché...Let's start over...It takes a dangerous street gang of invested creatives Shanghaied into free slave labor—to write a book, or a podcast, or anything worthwhile.

My personal creative pirate ship is populated by picaroons, good friends, family, dogs, and creative partners.

First, of course, thank you to my family for being the rock upon which my church is built, and without whose support nothing gets done! Yvonne, Katie, and Teresa—Love and devotion.

My podcast editors Dave, Duane, Tim, and Blake without whose tireless, (and usually last minute), ministrations the end product would be fraught with poor word choice, typos, and overindulgence.

Thanks guys. Long may you run.

Finally, thank you to the voice of the old man, Robert, who showed up every week and poured his heart and talent into making the story come alive. (www.commandvoices.com)

And anyone else who has lent a guiding hand, or a strong shove in the right direction along this journey.

With gratitude and love,

Chris

Table of Contents

Introduction

It was an overcast early morning in March of 2020. I had just started a new job and was attending a conference in Atlanta. There were dire and excited reports of a new virus sweeping the globe.

As was my habit I woke early in the hotel to get my run in. Looking at the online map I could see I wasn't far from the Chattahoochee River. In my years working in Atlanta, I always enjoyed running down by the 'Hooch'. It is a quiet spot beyond the reach of the city's frenetic bustle and roaring traffic.

I set off on a search for a trail from my hotel through a neighborhood that could get me there.

As I got into the morning adventure, I did find the neighborhood, and, after some searching, the trail. It led down a rain-slicked, sloping powerline to the banks of that constantly flowing stream.

And as I stood steaming in the morning mist an epiphany found me.

The new job, the swirling anxiety of the global pandemic, and my love of apocalyptic fiction came together in that moment and a bright vivid scene painted itself.

The old man.

The slippery trail.

The apocalypse.

I am used to ideas turning themselves into prose while I run, especially when I get off the roads and into the wilds. On this gray, dripping morning, a clear and irrevocable image of the old man, the river, and the apocalypse flashed into being and I fell in love with it.

C. S. Lewis, when asked how he conceived of the Narnia books and their beautiful fantasy and complex allegory, replied that it all started with an image. The image of a faun carrying an umbrella and parcels in a snowy wood. And from that single vivid image, the rest of it became as he started writing.

The image of the old man in the apocalypse was my version of this.

That night, on the plane I wrote a short story around that scene. I was, if not in love, at least infatuated.

My entire life I have been a reader of books. Truth be told, I've been a reader of anything that crosses my path, books, magazines, and an occasional cereal box. I love beautiful words and beautiful prose.

I have read hundreds of business books to augment my vocation in the search for knowledge. I have read my way through the classics on long plane rides. I hear the music in the words and feel the rhythms of good prose in my soul. It would be futile to attempt to list my influences.

They are legion.

Through all the reading and feeding the curiosity of my soul, the genre I hold close to as my particular guilty pleasure and vice is science fiction.

Why? Because science fiction is an imaginary place where real human consequences may be explored. Science fiction allows us to extend our realities into the 'what ifs' and that is where the good stuff happens.

For example, 'What if we drop this old man into the apocalypse?'

It has been a journey over the past five years writing my way through the After the Apocalypse universe across five seasons of the podcast. It hasn't always been easy or fun, but what lasting, important, relationships are?

Conflict, striving, loss, and rebirth are in everything human.

'What's this podcast?' you ask.

Picture a scene where fur-clad proto-humans cluster around a fire gnawing on mammoth bones. One of them stands up and begins to tell the story of the hunt! He or she gesticulates, and the pitch of the voice rises and lowers with the action. The audience is rapt, attentive, and engaged.

Storytelling is in our DNA, as is being a storyteller.

A podcast is simply that. Storytelling around the fire, except in this case there is a microphone instead of a bison humerus to chew on.

When I began to write the apocalypse story I heard the music of the words in my head. I felt the tone. I knew I would never be able to sit down and write an entire cohesive novel start to finish, (let alone five!) unless I gave myself an edge.

The podcast was that edge.

Every two weeks, I could produce a chapter, née episode, and engage talented voice artists to bring the music of the world to life as a story told. Over time, I would stack these written episodes up, one on top of the other, and at the end of the season, they would be the first draft of a manuscript for this book and the ones that are to follow.

And guess what? It worked.

This year, I will complete the fifth and final season of After the Apocalypse (www.oldmanapocalypse.com). And there, in the corner of my home office, will sit five dog-eared manuscripts—the first drafts of the five books in this series.

It is seldom in my life that a plan—especially one of this range and audacity—actually, well, '*goes to plan.*' But this one has. And I am tickled pink to present to you *After the Apocalypse: Book One – The Old Man*.

I hope you don't hate it, but at the end of the day, I have done my job. I have set this thing free. This thing that haunted me and forced itself into being on a drizzly morning on the banks of the Hooch.

The rest is entirely up to you,

Chris Russell

November 9th, 2024

Chapter One - The Old Man

November 21st – Three weeks since the virus ended the world...

The afternoon sun slanted warm across the river's surface. The water was high from the recent rains and a muddy hue swirled in the shallows. Early mayflies prickled the surface here and there, and lazy ripples hinted at fish and dorsal fins.

A cottonwood tree trailed its branches into the flow, creating a rip in the otherwise placid waters. In the low hiss of water sounds, a man cleared his throat.

"How long you been here?" the teenager asked.

Near an old shed by the water, an old man leaned back, cleared his throat, and spat. "A week or so now." He eyed the younger soul with a mix of weariness and caution.

The old man was just under six feet tall and lean, but not skinny. He wore an old pair of cargo shorts and a loose cotton work shirt.

It was hard to tell an exact age, but he was at least fifty years old, maybe older. He sported grey, longish hair, swept back, and held under a cap. His beard was grey-white with uneven patches of the original reddish brown standing like doomed islands in the flood of age.

He fixed the boy with sharp brown eyes.

The boy continued, leaning back onto a fallen tree, feigning disinterest, looking carefully sideways at the old man with shaded eyes. "You must've seen a lot in your time. What did you do before… yah know, before it happened?"

For the boy knew that the older ones liked to talk about the *before* times. Maybe he could get this surly old one off his guard.

"Yeah, I was there." The old man addressed part of the question and ignored the remainder carefully. He relaxed a bit and readjusted the weight of his wiry frame like a gymnast limbering up. "I was up north when it began. I worked my way down here where it's warmer, after the first wave hit."

"It got pretty weird." He continued. "Once the system got pushed beyond its limits, things got bad fast." He eyed the boy and gestured with a shrug to the top of a partially collapsed, burnt-out building tipping into the river less than a mile downstream.

"A lot of people died." He finished abruptly.

But the boy wouldn't let it rest and pulled the thread. "I heard up north there was the dying and then those who were left in the cities took to killin' each other."

The old man shrugged. "Once the supply chain broke down, it was a zero-sum game. Take a place like New York City, you had twenty to thirty thousand people per square mile and no way to keep them fed. Starving, dying people don't act reasonably." He looked out over the water. "It sorted itself out."

The boy looked over the man's shoulder, eyeing the shed and then the man himself. "What did you do back before, mister," the boy asked again.

A sharp look. "It doesn't matter, boy. I was fast and smart enough to make it out into the country and stay alive. We covered one hundred hard miles that first day and got out of the trouble. Those that couldn't run, stayed and died. We ran and lived." His eyes clouded over as he recalled the faces of ghosts.

The boy smoothed the front of his dirty shirt and casually moved his hand towards the hilt of his machete, as if brushing off a bit of dirt. "You got anything to trade, mister?"

The old man noted the boy's movement and squared himself. "I have some dried fish and squirrel, plus some sweet marsh plant that makes a pretty good stew. I'll feed you, kid. I have what I need here. But I'm not looking for company."

"I won't say no to a meal, mister. You've got a pretty good set-up here."

"I survive."

"Thanks, mister, let me cut some wood for a fire," the boy said, smiling, unsheathing the big blade and shouldering his way casually forward.

The old man rolled quickly over the log he was seated on, away from the boy. Landing on his feet, he took off running along the sandy shingle of the river.

"Come *back* here, you son of a bitch!" yelled the teenager, taking off in pursuit. But the old man already had a lead and was racing ahead.

The old man settled into a hard pace, his homemade sandals biting firmly into the soft mud. The boy was close on his heels, swearing and slipping.

A well-traveled trail opened on the left. The old man disappeared into the forest and up a steep, loose, rocky climb. The kid was pretty good and was staying close. Others might have given up at the sight of the big climb.

The old man stumbled on a round cobble in the path and wind-milled for balance. For a terrifying second or two, he thought he might not recover. If he fell, the kid would have him.

He was able to push off the hill with his hands and pistoned his legs to regain balance and keep moving, but the kid had gained some ground.

Nothing to be done for it now except to push like his life depended on it, because it probably did. Maybe he had underestimated the kid. Maybe this was the day when he'd have to stop running and fight.

The old man breathed deeply, filling his lungs, willing his heart to push blood down to soothe the burning in his thighs. He drove himself hard up the gravel slope, pumping his arms and lifting his complaining knees. The uphill was where he thought he had an advantage, so he pressed.

Three more stilted strides.

The fatigue in his quads felt like hot lead.

One last, deep, ungodly push and he was over the crest.

He shook out his arms and tried to will the pooling blood out of his legs. He sucked in a lungful of air and blew it out hard. He unfolded his lanky frame and dropped into the descent along, and then down the ridge.

He heard the kid about thirty feet back struggling up the loose slope. He relaxed his form and balanced his body against the downhill with long, quick strides, pulling his elbows back for balance.

He flew.

Through a cedar thicket and back out onto the river's bank, he pushed hard now for the shed. He rounded a corner and reached for where he knew it would be.

The kid was breathing hard when he came into view. He looked quite surprised, eyes wide in his dirty face as the old man settled his breathing and released the bolt from the crossbow.

It struck the boy cleanly in the chest. The boy staggered a couple more steps with his momentum and fell, a surprised look of pain and anger still on his face.

The old man scratched his scraggly beard and considered the kid laying on the ground, blowing bubbles of blood around the corners of his mouth.

It wouldn't be long now.

The old man hated to do it. He was supposed to save lives, not take them. But in this new world, after the apocalypse, the rules were different. It was every man for himself.

Even so, something old and familiar felt sick inside.

Should he even be feeling this regret? The kid could have let him go.

He'd much rather run than fight. He wasn't built for killing.

He was 99% sure that the kid was sent ahead to infiltrate his camp and catch him off guard. He saw it coming.

There had been tip-offs. The way the kid carried himself. The way he asked questions – the old man had seen it before.

Send the least threatening one in to test the situation and then the rest would come in to take advantage if there was an advantage to be taken.

In just a few weeks, the world seemed to have regressed into some sort of Machiavellian trench warfare and the Old Man needed to do what he had to do to survive. He didn't like it, but it was a matter of survival now.

Others might not have noticed the Trojan Horse nature of the boy's arrival in camp, but the old man did. It was his gift and his curse to be able to read people and see around corners to what was probably going to happen next. He wasn't always right, but he was right often enough that he'd learned to trust his instinct.

The kid had stopped breathing. Had gone to meet his ancestors and been added to the great pile of bones that was humanity's legacy. What did the old man care? Why should he mourn one more death on top of the millions of people who had recently been rubbed out of existence? Still, it bothered him. Sure, it was him or the kid — but what was so special about him? One old man surviving in the apocalypse. What did it even matter? One more day, one more week?

In the great chaotic calculus of the universe, maybe that kid deserved life more than the old man. Maybe he'd just snuffed out a future leader, a great savior who would rebuild this wreck of a world!

The old man shook himself out of his thoughts. *It was done*.

He wandered back into the shed he'd been squatting in and saw the old medals hanging on the wall. Some sort of race medals achieved by the previous resident. The old man had a box full of similar medals somewhere in a forgotten lifetime.

The old man considered it for a moment. He took a medal from the hook, stooped, and hung it around the boy's neck. He put his hand on the boy's forehead and uttered a swift prayer to his ancestors.

He asked for forgiveness.

Then he dragged the body to the river's edge and rolled it into the swiftly flowing stream.

Chapter Two - The Ford of Death

The old man looked around. The river, the smoke, the light drizzle, and the soft hump of the body making its way downstream to feed the rats of Atlanta.

He'd seen his share of death. He'd seen worse than this when he was in Africa and the Far East where, until not too long ago, death still stalked the muddy streets in the old ways. Disease. Warlords. Indiscriminate natural disasters and unfeeling politics. That's when he'd given up on humanity. Humanity was built on a despoiled pile of human bones, and he had given up. He'd ride out what was left of his life as a man *outside* that pile of bones.

He thought about an article he had read in an archeological magazine about a pile of bones they'd found in Kenya. These bones were over ten thousand years old. A small group of individuals were rounded up, slaughtered, and dumped in a pit. This was eight thousand years before Jesus and the Romans. The first traces of human activity were rife with internecine murder.

Before all this, he was at a point in his life where he mostly just wanted to be left alone.

He didn't miss the irony that he'd gotten his wish in this new world of the apocalypse. Turns out, he didn't have to abandon humanity. They had left on their own. Humanity was back to the level of ten thousand years ago with roaming bands and small groups looking to survive, and murder was as good an option as any.

For the past few years, since he had returned from Africa, the old man had been a vagabond. He tramped around the country, living off the kindness of others and running long-distance events.

He could no longer practice medicine in this country.

He was estranged from his family and any friends he had from his old life as a doctor.

He found the ultra-running community to be indifferent to all of this. These people were trail bums who hiked or ran the long trails. A bunch of ex-addicts, hippies, and dysfunctional adults who lived to spend their days pounding out their lives on the forest trails of America.

They were all running away from something. The forest didn't ask any questions.

The old man wasn't as old as he looked or pretended to be. He found it useful to fade into the background, to appear non-threatening in this world. If the scraps of humanity haunting this place knew his real capabilities, it might become inconvenient and dangerous.

At just under six feet tall, the old man was not imposing. He didn't look like the athlete he was. Skinny and balding with a slight pot belly, no one would suspect that he was one of the top endurance athletes in his age group. Perhaps if they looked closer at the ropy muscles twitching under the loose skin of his thighs they might wonder — but they never did.

Turns out, being tough and able to move long distances on foot was pretty much the job description of a survivor in the apocalypse. He'd retired from real life a few years back anyhow, so it really didn't make any difference to him. He'd written them all off. He'd seen this as inevitable.

He just wasn't expecting it in *his* lifetime.

The old man shook his head and spat into the muddy grass beside the river. He'd have to move. This place was too much on the beaten path out of the city. From the beginning of time, people had followed the rivers. They were the highways of humanity. If he wanted to avoid humanity, he'd have to find a different route.

He put his light pack together and stood, straightening with a groan.

Squinting upriver, he thought he saw some movement. A mangy group of two-legged beasts emerged from around the bend. He had wanted to continue south anyhow. But had hoped to avoid following the river through the city.

They saw him and yelled something. Looked like two of them. Maybe more. Men. It was usually men now. The women tended to hunker down, to look for a place to hold up, to ride out the storm. But for some reason, men became unhinged and wanted to keep moving. *'Maybe some deep-rooted hunter-gatherer instinct'* he thought.

He turned and began to move. A slow jog to warm up his old legs and get the blood moving again.

His pursuers picked up their pace and closed ground. He took a drink from his bottle and a bite of jerky from a pocket in his shorts.

He stretched it out a little, enlivening the pace to what he thought should do the trick. The group behind him stopped running and started walking with some more shouts and protestations.

***

One of the many ironies in his life was that he had been a bookish, chubby, non-athletic kid. Always studying. Never any time for sports, which he considered the games of lesser boys and men. He had come to the sport of ultra-distance running late in life, when his career as a doctor was over.

He had needed something to keep him moving. Something to help him forget. The physical pain of these multi-hour, multi-day running events had kept him alive.

He notched his pace down and looked around to see where the sun was now. It was low and to his left, so he was running south. He would put twenty miles between him and his pursuers by the end of the day, but usually, only the first mile mattered.

The old man began singing an old country song that had popped into his head. Something about the evils of liquor and whorehouses. That made him laugh. Turns out, when someone bioengineered a new virus, it was just a little bit *more* evil than those moral sins—and there probably wasn't a song about that.

There was a car in the river ahead. He slowed to let the panorama paint itself. He had learned to do this – to slow down and make sure he was seeing the whole scene. By default, he let his mind drift and become unfocused when he was running alone in the woods. Sometimes he had to mentally slap himself back into awareness.

If one wanted to survive, one was best served by being mentally present and alert in the apocalypse. He stopped for a moment and surveyed the scene. It was afternoon now. The sun was higher. There was the sound of birds and the low wet sounds of the river making its timeless way like General Sherman to the sea.

Nothing much to see here. The wrecked car, partially submerged, seemed to have come from the overpass above. That plunge was probably enough to kill the driver. Some sick person in the throes of death trying to make a break for it. Or maybe a suicide.

One more scene of commonplace carnage in the apocalypse.

One more bag of bones for humanity's piles of bones.

He knew about bones. He knew about blood. He knew most of what made the fragile human body work. Not because he was some sort of macabre ghoul, but because he *had* been a doctor. One of the best. Top of his class.

Coveted residency. The culmination of all that studying and what he thought was his dream.

He had married young and had kids, because that's what you did when you were a renowned physician. You did that so no one could accuse you of being a self-centered careerist with a God complex.

It was in the playbook.

He felt a stab of pain, a twinge of guilt as he thought of the mousey young woman in his wedding bed and the two young heads in his Long Island study. He shook his head. Water under the bridge. He couldn't change any of it and he didn't want to.

All these people. His wife. His kids. His colleagues. Those men futilely chasing him. The poor sod in the crashed car. The Paleolithic wanderers with their heads smashed in, thrown into that long-ago pit in the rift valley - all bones on the pile of bones that was humanity's legacy.

He'd quit the game. They couldn't get him anymore. He wasn't playing. Humanity was no longer his problem. If they wanted to die or live or kill each other in the apocalypse, he could care less. His life was his forward motion. He was waiting for death with open arms when death came for him to take his bones.

But the truth was that the old man had one more thing to do in this dead life of his. He wouldn't admit it to himself, but he did have a center of gravity that was pulling him south and west. There was one son unaccounted for. There was one loose thread tying the old man still to this dead world.

Whether or not he wanted to come out and admit it, he was being pulled by a simple question. One he feared he already knew the answer to. His thinking brain was afraid to give this ghost a tacit form. The simple ghost of a question was, *what had happened to his youngest son, Paul?*

The old man resumed his shuffling pace, looking now for a way to turn west. West was where he was going. There were a handful of states between here and there. Some small mountains and some wilderness.

He would make his way. He always did. The key to survival was to keep moving—to keep *running*.

Chapter Three - Home and Castle

The old man pushed on as the dirt road turned away from the river and drifted westward. That was a plus because he really didn't want to go into the city.

Still, he was on the outskirts of the great sprawl of Atlanta. There were more buildings here, not directly on the dirt road but visible through the pine trees draped with kudzu.

Clouds had blown in from the south, bringing a slow drizzle from the faraway Gulf. "The sweat of coupling crawdads," he chuckled, paraphrasing an old science saying that "in every raindrop was contained the sweat of your parents' coupling." The concept was that all the water molecules on Earth were recycled infinitely.

The red dirt kicked up and coated his bare legs as his feet maintained their steady pat, pat, pat. That wasn't good. He was leaving tracks now; tracks that could be followed. But it couldn't be helped. He wasn't going to thrash about in the muddy undergrowth to avoid the road. He'd never get anywhere.

The rainwater was starting to drip from the brim of his cap now. He'd have to be careful since it was getting muddy. When that wet Georgia clay turned into muck, it was like running in marzipan paste.

The old man adjusted the straps on his backpack. The pack held whatever food he could scrounge. From experience, he knew he could live on just about anything. The other runners had a saying; *"If the furnace is hot enough anything will burn."*

The pack also had a bladder that carried a liter of water when full.

He tried to limit what he carried. He valued the ability to cover distance more than the surety of having stuff. But he had collected what he needed to survive on the run. There was a multitool, a raincoat, a lighter for fires, a blanket, a small tent, and a tarp – all crammed tightly into the pack and balanced for running so it wouldn't bounce around.

A knife hung from his belt on the side and his crossbow hooked above the pack where he could reach it if he had to.

From the heft of the pack, he could tell that his food situation was currently running on the lean side. He'd been rushed out of his camp before he could provision.

He'd need to remedy that.

Up ahead the old man saw a parking area off the dirt road. As he came upon it, he saw that it was a trailhead. Not a dirt road or a forest trail, but one of those paved, rails-to-trails pathways.

A large sign stood braced by two stout pressure-treated uprights. The sign had a hinged door with a plexiglass window. The plexiglass had been scratched up with initials and other graffiti; apparently, some local teens were infatuated enough to commit minor vandalism in the name of budding love.

Framed in the big window, behind the graffiti, along with various announcements forbidding off-leash dogs and motor vehicles, was a map of the trail. This was promising.

The old man traced his finger west from the orange 'You are here' sticker all the way to Tennessee. It looked like this trail could get him through the mountains and into the Ohio Valley.

He fought back a shiver as the rainwater ran down the back of his shirt. With the rain coming down and the day getting late, he should be looking for somewhere to camp for the night. From the trailhead, he thought he could see some houses further up the road and splashed off through the red mud to investigate.

It must have been a nice neighborhood, back when such things mattered. The houses were large and set on generous chunks of land positioned away from each other. Red brick mansions with vines climbing the walls set back from the road in wooded hollows. Quite nice for some local doctors, lawyers, or politicians.

The old man pushed open a wrought iron gate that was set into two ten-foot, fieldstone pillars. A stone wall capped with mortar and more wrought iron work ran around the periphery of the property. Some concrete bulldogs sat atop the pillars. Someone was sending a clear message that they didn't want the hoi polloi wandering about on their land. Georgia had always been obsessed with property rights. And the bulldogs were the emblem of its favorite university.

He walked carefully down the flagstone path to the house, feeling a bit like a cat burglar. Even in the apocalypse, he felt like he was trespassing, committing a transgression on property rights. But he knew that he certainly wasn't a bandit, and if anyone was here, he'd get the hell out.

Like it or not, the human body wanted to be warm and dry when it could, and like it or not, as efficient a runner as he was, he still burned calories and needed to keep fueling. He needed to seek shelter and to re-provision.

The old man left the path and worked his way through a gap in the hedges to the side of the house where there was a stone patio. The rain bounced in puddles between the stones and gave the wicker furniture a slick sheen. Such nice furniture. Shame it would probably be gone in a season, rotted, or used to make a fire.

The old man considered dragging one of these benches under the covering trees to make a bed for himself, but knew he had to check out the house first. Chances were quite good that there were no survivors in there. There seldom were.

He pressed his face up against the porch door windows, after carefully wiping a patch clean of rainwater. He didn't see anything moving in there, but there were the telltale marks of flies on the window. Flies trapped and full of human flesh and looking to get out.

The old man wasn't afraid of bodies. Death didn't scare him. He'd seen too much of it in his life, both professionally and personally to be bothered by human carcasses. But, on a purely primal level, he couldn't choke back all the disgust.

At this point, three weeks in, the bodies were really starting to decompose. The flesh of the corpses was greenish or red and some were horribly bloated.

He didn't mind the bodies, but he also didn't want to spend time with them. That smell of death was hard to get out of your clothes. He remembered it well from his time in Africa.

He wasn't afraid of contagion either. As near as he could figure he had already had this bug, or a close relative of it, while he was overseas, and he guessed that he had some sort of immunity. It struck him as ironic that his being banished by the leading men of his profession out into a third-world Doctors Without Borders practice would end up protecting him from *their* fate.

As near as he could tell the virus had struck hard and fast. It seemed like everyone got sick at the same time, which was unusual. Usually, a virus would take hold and spread, but this one seemed to come out of nowhere and be everywhere at once.

He knew he had probably been exposed. He'd been around the sick and had tried to help them. But he never even got a sniffle.

The great, lonely, ironic privilege of being the last man alive. Like some Hollywood drama. Except he wasn't the last person alive. And he had to pay attention to that fact as he tried the latch and pushed the door open.

The soiled, stale, greasy smell of death greeted him. Nothing could be done about it now. He pushed in and pulled up his scarf, wrapping it around his face.

The first body looked like it had once been the patriarch of the household. He was face down by the front door, having apparently made one last try to get out of the house. Why? To safety? Was he going to drive to a hospital? Was he going to work? To see his mistress?

Whatever his goal, he hadn't made it.

There were others in the bedrooms, entombed in soiled sheets and blankets.

The old man said a quick prayer for the dead despite having given up on religion many years ago. But it just felt right. He found that he didn't need to believe in God to find comfort in the ceremony of prayer. He closed the bedroom doors and walked down the hall to the kitchen.

"Time to see what the good people of this castle have for sustenance," he said out loud to no one, needing to hear his own voice just then.

In the pantry, he found some cans of beans, cans of tuna, and some other assorted things that he stacked neatly in his pack. He hefted the pack and thought about having that bouncing against his back for the next one hundred miles with a grimace. He stuffed a couple of long boxes of spaghetti into the pack, to keep the cans away from his shoulder blades, and settled the pack back into position.

Next, the old man went to the fridge, knowing that there probably wasn't anything in there that was still good, but not being able to resist the urge to open it anyway. The pulse of bad air from the decomposing contents was almost as bad as the odor coming from the deceased occupants of the house.

He was delighted to see a couple of bottles of high-end beer in the back and stuffed them into his vest pockets. He knew he needed to keep his wits about him, but two beers wouldn't hurt and he could use the carbs to fuel his run.

He left the kitchen and moved back through the family room, looking around to see if anything else might be useful.

There, on the mantle above a stone fireplace, was a picture of the family. A balding, middle-aged man in a suit. A dumpy, smiling wife. And three beaming sons, all in holiday sweaters, next to a robustly decorated Christmas tree. He looked at the picture and looked around. It was taken in front of this very hearth.

The old man reached out with his wet hand, picked the picture up, and examined it. What were they thinking when that photo was taken? Had she set the photo shoot up? Nagged the boys to get dressed up? Had they dragged their feet and complained until she promised to cook their favorite meal?

He put the picture back, considered it, straightened it, and turned to head down the hall out through the mud room to the attached garage.

He would have grabbed a blanket or a towel to dry off, but they all smelled like death. He knew from experience that once death got into your clothes and hair it would stick with you for days. Before opening the door to the garage, he checked to make sure he hadn't left obvious muddy footprints that would betray his visit. He couldn't see anything to worry about in that regard and continued.

Closing and latching the connecting door to the garage, he pulled away his scarf and took a couple of long breaths. The air was dry and tinged with the metallic smell of oil, but it was better than the smell of rotting death that filled the house.

There were bicycles hung on the walls and a beautiful Cadillac Escalade parked in the single bay. He thought about that. He could very well find the keys and take this tank of a car for a ride, but he didn't like that idea. Cars attracted too much attention. They were limited to the roads. The roads were dangerous now.

Nice big car though. He could sleep in it quite comfortably. But, after slowing down to take in the whole scene he saw there was an attic or loft accessible by a pull-down door.

He climbed the rickety ladder stairs up into the loft and looked around at the dry storage space. It was perfect. He pulled himself and drew the stairs up behind him. It was getting dark now.

There were some old blankets up here. Maybe the kids had used it as a fort. He knew if he was a boy growing up in this house, he'd have used it as a fort.

He hung some bits of his kit up to dry and wrapped a blanket around his shoulders. He popped the cap off a bottle and drank a nice big swig of the warm beer. He wiped his mouth, satisfied, and settled down to sleep.

The rain tapped on the roof above him and dripped off the eaves. It smelled a bit like a barn, with the open woodwork overhead.

It was dark now. He was dry. He was warm. It didn't get any better in the apocalypse.

But in this new world, he wasn't safe. He was never safe.

Chapter Four - Home Invasion

The old man was awakened by the sound of men shouting. It took him a minute to shake off the haze and remember where he was. He had to pee but that would have to wait.

"Nothing in the basement!" a man shouted from the house.

"Check the garage!" Another shouted back from further away. "The tracks led this way. He was here. Watch yourself."

The garage door below was flung open, followed by the sound of feet shuffling and circling the Escalade. The old man could hear the first man breathing and the rustle of his clothing.

The other had caught up and, from the garage door asked, "Anything? Did you check the car?"

"Yeah, nice ride, but nothing in there."

"Crap. I thought we might have surprised him by pushing through the night. Did you look under the car?"

There were some more shuffling and clothing noises and a grunt. "Nuthin' under the car." A long pause. "What do you think?"

"I think I want to teach that guy a lesson, but we gotta catch him first."

"Moved pretty fast for an old guy. Hey, I know you're pissed but maybe we should cut our losses and head into the city."

"No, we'll find him. We'll get him eventually; how would *you* feel if he killed *your* brother? You wouldn't want to give up so easily then, would yah?"

"Ok, OK," the first man said, "Let's clear this place out, load up what we can, and see if we can find the keys to this rig. Maybe rack out here for the night."

"It will be nice to be dry and off our feet for a couple of hours," the second agreed.

The garage door closed behind them, and they went back into the house. The old man let out a breath he hadn't realized he was holding. These people were persistent. Persistent and homicidal.

He reasoned that the best move now was to wait them out. They didn't know he was here. On the other hand, he was trapped. He could try to risk climbing down and sneaking out, but could he do that without being seen and caught? No. He would hide here until they were gone. But that didn't help the fact that he still had to pee. Looking around, he saw the empty beer bottle and was relieved.

Over the next thirty minutes, the old man quietly gathered his things about him and prepared as best he could to either fight or flee if they discovered him. He quietly pulled on his shoes and tightened them. He made sure his crossbow was armed and handy.

He considered his options. How were these two able to catch up to him? They must have found some transportation or hiked all night in the cold rain. That made them focused and mad—and dangerous.

His best bet was to wait them out up here in the rough loft above the garage. If they hadn't found him by now, they probably wouldn't.

A guy he knew from one of the clubs that he ran with once said, "If you can run, run. If you can't run...learn *how* to run." The joke was that if you were a runner, you could probably solve just about any problem by running. But in this case, the smarter play was to have patience.

He listened as they ransacked the house, swearing and breaking things. He thought about the holiday photo of the family on the fireplace mantle. That was just another memory among millions of others that would fade now. Fade into the past. Broken and forgotten.

The men made several trips to the garage, loading boxes into the Escalade. They had found the keys and started the car, discovering to their satisfaction that it had a full tank of gas. They shut it off until they were ready to leave.

One of them, the alpha, was named Rod. The other was Johnny. They talked a bit about the chaos and the killing. They didn't seem to have much of a plan, other than to survive and take what they needed.

The sun was shining in through the slats in the aluminum vent at the end of his attic space. It was getting warm when they finally slammed the doors of the big car and got ready to leave. They had to figure out how to manually open the big garage door, now that the power was out.

The old man lay silent, eyeing them through a very small crack between the plywood boards.

After they pulled the Caddie out, one of them ran back in and grabbed a gas can and containers of oil from the metal shelves. '*Good idea to have the extra gas*', the old man thought.

They would be gone soon enough. Probably making their way into the city with that big car, to see what trouble they could get into there. Maybe they'd given up on him.

When it was safe, the old man would slip from his hiding place, backtrack to that rail trail, and head north and west into Tennessee.

The two men stopped the car in the driveway and did something he couldn't discern before driving off. He figured he'd give them twenty minutes or so, just to make sure. No sense hurrying. He didn't have any appointments.

The sun warmed his space. The cicadas buzzed in the trees outside. It could have been any other afternoon nap for the old man. He laid his head on one arm and dozed.

***

It might have been twenty minutes. It might have been more when he was roused by the smell of smoke. It came curling up through the cracks in the plywood like dirty, evil fingers and choked him.

They had enacted a final act of violence on this castle. A pyre for the dead.

He had to get out. And he had to get out fast.

He could feel the heat and hear the fire now spreading quickly from the house. Like a hungry animal, it raced through the structure as if looking for him.

He pushed down on the retractable ladder but was greeted by a staggering blast of heat and acrid smoke as soon as there was a gap. The open garage was acting like a chimney, and the fire was hungry in this old wood structure.

The old man pushed his way back, away from the main fire in the house and towards the other end of the attic, pulling his scarf up over his nose and mouth.

He frantically pulled and pushed at the vent in the eave, clawing at the screws and wire. He was choking on the smoke. He had to get out or he would die.

He had his knife out and was working at the screws around the vent grate.

"Come *on...!*" He cursed, the knife slipping into the stripped screw heads.

It wasn't working.

At this rate, he'd be dead before the first screw was loose.

In a panic, he lay back and mule-kicked at the vent. He managed to break a couple of slats free. He worked to squeeze his shoulders through the opening. The fire was coming closer and roared behind him, its hot fingers grabbing at him with hungry malice.

He tossed out his pack and tried again to squeeze through. He was pushing and clawing with all his might to get through the rough opening he had kicked out.

He was stuck, thrashing, halfway out, his belt stuck on the edge. At least there was less smoke outside where his head was now, and he could breathe.

He filled his lungs with fresh air, exhaled deeply, and made one last great heave. He popped free of the vent and plummeted to the thick grass of the lawn.

Scrambling, and a bit in shock, he ran hunched over for the tree line in the backyard. He settled behind a big oak and watched the scene. The flames leaped high into the noon sky with black smoke. Surely this would attract some attention. He needed to get out of here.

He had almost died, stuck halfway out the window. He was reminded of an old photo he had seen. Maybe in Time or Life magazine. Of a dead man who had been trying to escape from a burning house. Maybe in Africa. Frozen by the photographer's eye with one arm and shoulder out from under the house, but dead from the fire within.

More evidence of man's reckless violence against man. More bones for the pile. But this day, he had made it, now he had to shake off the shock of it and get out of there.

He didn't see anyone else around. Although the roaring fire made it hard to see much. He shouldered his pack and hugged the tree line through the backyard to get back to the road.

Then he saw the big black Escalade parked in the road out front. What were they doing? Admiring their handiwork? Or trying to smoke him out. Either way, he had to move before they saw him. He would have to pass close to the road to get by.

The old man stayed low and went from the covering safety of one tree to the next. He was making his way back towards the trailhead. Once he got there, he could head away from this place quickly and put some space between himself and these arsonists.

He thought he was out of danger, just one hundred feet from the entrance to the trailhead parking area when he heard the Escalade engine start and the sound of tires spinning from acceleration.

He broke into a sprint, or the best version of a sprint that he could conjure. As experienced a runner as he was, there is a big difference between distance and speed. He could stay on his feet for a hundred-mile race but didn't have as much talent for short sprints. He did not look over his shoulder, but he could hear the car coming down the road towards him and accelerating. He could sense the pursuit.

He put his head down and gave it all he had. The last of the smoke was well cleared from his lungs and he was breathing hard as he willed his legs to move faster. Adrenaline was pumping and his heart was pounding with fear like a hunted animal.

He made the turn into the dirt parking area and made for the trail.

He couldn't outrun a car, but he could get on the other side of the trailhead barrier, and they would have a hard time following.

The barrier was two thick steel posts, anchored in cement footings. It allowed foot traffic but prevented vehicles.

He heard the gravel flying and the wheels of the Escalade spinning in the dirt of the parking area as they careened in right behind him.

The old man could run for hours at his usual pace, but he could not keep up his current sprint for much longer. He put his head down and funneled every remaining bit of energy he had into the metal barrier just feet ahead of him.

The Escalade wasn't slowing down. They fish-tailed through the parking area and accelerated toward the gate behind him. They were almost on him. He could hear the hungry engine like a grizzly bear on his heels.

One final push of superhuman effort dredged from the bottom of his overworked adrenal glands and he dove headlong through the metal pipes into the trail.

The Escalade impaled itself on the steel gate with a terrible crunch. Even with its size and velocity, it couldn't breach the barrier. It hung on the pipes with its engine racing and the back wheels spinning off the ground.

The old man rolled to his feet and resumed his flight down the trail.

A quick glance at the Escalade revealed nothing but deployed airbags behind a cracked windshield. Maybe some left-over automated voice was asking them if they had been in an accident and needed assistance.

He wasn't going to stay and find out.

He was one hundred feet further down the trail when he saw the dirt kick up by his feet and heard gunshots. He ran an improvised zigzag for another fifty feet until he could get around a bend in the trail and out of sight.

He slowed his pace and walked a bit, to recover and let the adrenaline drain from his system. He did a quick scan of his body, and nothing seemed broken or hurt. He'd probably have some sore spots tomorrow. But that wasn't much of a bill to pay, considering all the excitement.

It was a close call.

He could have died today.

Those men wanted to kill him. That fire wanted to kill him. This world wanted him to die. But he was still here and still moving.

The old man felt a twinge of pride at that. He was a survivor. He may have given up on this world, but he wasn't a man you could brush off so easily. He could run. He could survive. Maybe there was something in this world for him. Maybe there was some sort of purpose.

It wasn't like he had a choice in the matter. He'd keep moving and see what this dirty and dead world brought.

If he managed to survive a few more days, he might make it to Paul. That's all he had now.

Survive.

Survive and *move.*

Stack one day on top of the next and see where this world went.

Chapter Five - Killer

November 21st – Three weeks since the virus ended the world…

Her name was Janet Kramer, but her coworkers called her "KJ".

She didn't know why.

She supposed it didn't matter anymore.

She was shell-shocked and confused. Just trying to make any kind of sense out of what had happened over the last two weeks since the virus struck.

Trying to survive.

Running from the city.

If Janet was going to survive, she would need to use those hard skills she had cultivated over the years and put soft things aside.

"KJ," she mused as the big Five-liter V8 purred down the abandoned highway. That was the devious beauty of a perfect nickname. When the recipient of the nickname didn't know, but suspected, there was something else going on. Some subtle dig. Some backhanded comments about her personality that the perpetrators could deny.

As far as she could tell the "K" stood for "Killer", but she hadn't figured out the "J" just yet. She had her suspicions.

But now she'd probably never know for sure.

It was just part of the gauntlet she had to run every day.

The talking heads liked to opine about how empowered professional women were – how they were leaders in these modern, enlightened times. Indeed, the partners in her firm had trotted her out as an example every time the subject came up.

But the old biases were still there. Like water forced underground. Lurking under the surface like a pent-up geyser.

The male partners and associates were jealous of her abilities, and she had to be twice as good. The jealousy even seemed to have gotten worse when it was against the rules to *overtly* attack her. When it had no way to express itself, no way to vent. Those rules, meant to protect, only amplified the spite by making her a protected species.

Instead, they had played their petty games and had fun with their subtle jabs. The snide remarks, and now the nickname, had been a covert way to push back. They hadn't been able to beat her in the open, so they had hidden in the bushes and thrown mud, so to speak.

She smiled a bit at that visual, her perfect white canine teeth emerging from hard, thin lips in the mirror, just for a moment before she caught herself. Little men, cowering in bushes throwing mud, like little, spiteful gremlins. She liked that image.

She wasn't one to just smile and accept it. Her rivals had learned that. But she still had to be careful which hills she chose to die on. She had preferred to set the agendas, drive the cases, make things happen, and not respond to petty jabs from petty boys whose feelings had been hurt or who felt threatened.

Those pricks. The jerks in her office. Hard-charging guys with nice suits and bad habits.

She smiled slightly again, "They're probably all dead now."

And she wasn't.

But what now?

She had gotten sick like everyone else. For days she had languished in their apartment, with her husband and children, each of them succumbing to the sickness before her, but she didn't give in. She forced herself to eat and drink, to stay alive. And after a while, she knew she would survive, she always did.

When she woke up from her sickness, her family was gone. She didn't know how long she had been out of it. A few hours? A few days?

She tried to call 911 but there was no signal. She tried to turn on the TV, but the power was out. She sat in the dark apartment wondering what to do. Her family was dead. The apartment was starting to reek of their death. She had to get out of there. She could get away from the city. Drive somewhere safe. Wait for this crisis to be over and return when it was safe to take care of her loved ones.

There was a good view of the city from their apartment. She could see the destruction - fires, smoke, wrecks, bodies. It didn't look like it was getting better as her sick days dragged on. A few things still occasionally moved in her field of view, but nothing that gave her hope. Nothing that pointed to an impending recovery.

She made her decision. She tucked the bodies of her family into their beds, weeping painfully as she did so. She closed the bedroom doors behind her, sealing off those remnants of her life.

Leaning on the walls for support and crying she locked the apartment and made her way slowly down the stairwell to the street.

When she had recovered enough to drag herself out of her building, it was all chaos. There were cars smashed in the road like some farcical demolition derby. It seemed like half the city was on fire. There were gunshots and shouting...but strangely no sirens.

Worst of all, there were dead and dying everywhere. It was like some medieval nightmare - some old painting of the Inquisition with demons pulling the flesh from the screaming penitent.

That reinforced her decision. She knew she had to get out of the city.

Her family was gone. She couldn't change that.

Winners don't cry, they take control and make things happen; so, she pulled herself into her red Land Rover and headed out of town. She would get out of the city and head south. She would drive to her parents and the small-town safety of their house to ride out this storm.

Now, here she was driving away from her loss, gripping the steering wheel and fighting to stay conscious despite her exhaustion. Looking bleary-eyed through the tears into a weirdly dark night.

The lines on the road flashed by and she started to fade from consciousness again, caught herself, and focused.

She was from the south. That was another thing that made those boys mad. With their clipped "Eastern standard" accents bred from those years of lacrosse and liberal arts at places like Andover and Groton. The prep boys heard a twinge of a Southerner in your voice and assumed you were soft as a morning biscuit.

She quickly taught them differently. She used their biases against them. She smiled her polite debutant smile as they impaled themselves on their own cultural absurdities. They never learned.

Another thing about Janet that made them uncomfortable was her size and athletic physique.

At six ft tall she made an impression in every meeting. She was a physical presence that could not be ignored. She didn't shy away from it. She used it to her advantage.

Even after college, she had continued to keep her body tuned.

Even after marriage.

Even after the kids came.

Even with the work at the law practice dragging long days out of her.

She continued to work out and stay strong. She pursued fitness like she pursued everything else.

She hunted it down and made it hers.

It was a harrowing drive out of the city. There were wrecked cars off the road, cars burning, or just abandoned randomly on the road. There were people, dead and almost dead.

At first, she had tried to avoid the corpses on the road. Eventually, she came to see them as inconveniences. She still slowed down and did her best to drive around, but when all else failed the Range Rover had the clearance to go over and through the dead. She wasn't even sure if this was really happening. If it wasn't a hallucinatory aspect of the sickness that had so recently clutched at her.

There were bodies still moving. Some tried to get her to stop.

She had pressed the accelerator hard and grimaced as a shambling survivor tried to flag her down.

What were they thinking? How was she supposed to help anyone? The loss of her family and the ravages of the disease had scraped away at her empathy.

She could barely stay upright herself. She had to get out of the city. She didn't have the energy reserves to take on someone else's problems. Hadn't she suffered enough? They could fend for themselves like she did.

When she eased onto the interstate and things looked relatively clear, Janet took a deep breath of the leather-smelling air and reached for the bottle of water.

She took a long swig and swallowed. She choked a bit and coughed hard into a napkin. The napkin revealed dark green phlegm tinged with blood. She swallowed hard to clear her throat. It was still a bit raw. Her lungs still rattled when she breathed. But it was getting better.

She tossed the napkin to the passenger side floor. It was an orange-brown color with dancing skeletons and cartoon zombies on it. Leftover from Halloween.

Ironic. A cartoon celebration of death. The real thing wasn't quite as amusing.

Jeez, this world with its constant ironies.

With the kids, she made a habit of hoarding napkins in the car. They were always spilling something. These napkins were from the high-end coffee shop she patronized with the kids on weekends while she gave her husband Jim a break. Friends would joke that they were like a divorced couple, and she got the kids on the weekends.

The thought of her family brought a wave of melancholy so strong that she almost lost control. She had to jerk the wheel to stay on the road. She had been at it for hours now and it was dark. She was weak and tired and knew she would have to take a rest eventually.

More irony, she thought. Janet Kramer, the woman who never rested, now needed badly to rest.

With every mile she put between herself and the death behind her, she also felt a sense of freedom. One that made her feel stronger but also pulled at a strand of guilt and sadness for what she had lost.

She pressed on down the road until the Range Rover started to run low on gas. *Crap!* She'd have to find some gas, diesel actually.

She knew the gas stations were probably a bad idea. She thought she remembered that most stations had run out of gas quickly when people started dying. Something about that was on the news before the TV went out. Something about the pumps not having power to work when the grid came down.

She was busy at the time trying to keep her husband and kids alive as they coughed and choked to death in her arms. They didn't even recognize her near the end in their delirium. Her husband screamed for his mother and wept between gasps like an abandoned child.

She had tried. God, she had tried! But what could she do? She tried to get them to drink soup and put cold, wet towels on their foreheads. She cleaned them up. She made frantic calls for help until the network failed.

Janet Kramer, the best damn lawyer in the business, unbeatable, the "Killer". She could make most things bend to her will, but she couldn't pull her own family out of the jaws of this horror.

She watched them die. *Helpless* to change it.

She wasn't a doctor. She was the one who took down doctors. The malpractice specialist. She went after those corporate jerkoffs who made bad decisions and hurt people. She brought them down to earth. *She hurt them*.

The irony again.

Where were those doctors now? Where were those medical corporations with their grand plans to change the world? Those devious plans that always promised a grand future while harvesting money through wrongful death in the present? This new bug had done more to cut them down than she ever could.

When the bug finally got her, it ravaged her body like an express train. Fever. Chills that shook her whole body and made her bones ache. Throwing up blood. Coughing so hard she thought her insides would just fall out of her throat. It got to a point where a lesser person, without her strength, would wish for death just to get away from it.

And most did.

But she didn't.

"Why?" she cried out plaintively and pounded the steering wheel once with her open palm. *Why did she survive when her loved ones did not?*

Probably because she was tough. Tough and strong. She was one of the strongest people she knew. She worked hard, long days at the practice but she also carved out time for fitness.

She had stayed in shape. She was strong and hard and tough, and that might be why she was still here, pushing this British-made car down the road.

Jogging or aerobics classes with the city hausfraus was not her speed. She needed something more intense to burn off the mental and physical stress of her job. Early-morning CrossFit and Krav Maga classes kept her hard and lean. It fit her personality to unleash torrents of physical energy like water from a high-pressure dam, throwing the other student to the mat.

She was a fighter. That's why she survived.

The gas light on the dash was on now. She needed to find fuel.

She eased off an exit that promised a shopping district. It was quiet here. She didn't see any other cars moving. It was eerie. She eased through the stop lights that no longer worked, but swung above the road like silent gatekeepers, and made her way toward the big box stores.

She'd need to siphon. She remembered how to do it from her childhood in rural South Carolina. She needed a gas can, maybe more than one. She needed a length of hose. Then she had to find some vehicles without the antitheft devices and siphon some diesel.

She had a bad feeling about this. In her weakened state she was worried about leaving the car. But she'd have to do it if she wanted to keep going. *Besides,* she thought, *the worst of the chaos was probably isolated to the city. Out here in the suburbs, things should be better.*

She pulled into a super-store parking lot and circled around back to the loading docks. No sense in being too visible and attracting unwanted attention. She knew this could be the point where, even with all her strength and skill, she should avoid interacting.

With some reservation she parked the car behind a dumpster, manually locking the doors.

She resisted using the key fob lock because it would make that beeping noise. She pocketed the fob and started her approach to the store.

She was nervous. She wobbled unsteadily on weakened legs looking furtively around the parking lot at the back of the store. Nothing moved except scraps of windblown trash. She stumbled slightly. She realized that she had stepped awkwardly on a half-crushed soda can.

Janet felt a small panic rise in her gut. Like she was walking into something she couldn't control. Something unknown.

But then, like clockwork, a switch flipped in her mind the way it always did when something hard needed to be done.

Life requires risk, Janet Kramer reminded herself. *Everything is going to be ok.*

She straightened up and moved forward.

Chapter Six - Anarchy

Janet glanced back at the nose of the Range Rover sticking out from behind the dumpster.

She regretted having to leave it. It had become the center of her world since fleeing the city.

A safe harbor. A den-like space, comfortable and familiar, where *she* had control.

It couldn't be helped. She needed fuel. She needed food and supplies.

She walked past the back doors and loading docks, and turned the corner to the outdoor gardening and landscape area of the big box store, looking for a way to get in. On a gate that blocked the entrance to a large, chain-link fenced area, a sign read "Yard and Garden."

If there were gas cans and garden hoses, they'd be down at this end of the store, but how would she get to them? The store was obviously closed. There was no one here.

Should she try to break in?

She was who she was. The moral certainty of fifteen years of law practice wasn't going to go away easily. She was, frankly, conflicted about breaking into this store.

At this point, the dark dreamscape of fleeing the city seemed like it might have happened to someone else. She remembered the bodies on the road, the sick people, and the burning buildings with broken windows.

But she hadn't managed to process it quite yet.

With the sickness still lingering in her and the adrenaline of the drive, how much of that was real? She still wasn't thinking clearly.

Was that just an isolated riot confined to the city? Was that a momentary burp in the civil fabric that cities experienced once in a while, when under duress from outside forces? Like Watts or Chicago? Terrible convulsions of violence that would peak in an awful orgy of chaos, but then burn out and subside?

It couldn't be like that everywhere, could it? Even out here in suburbia?

The store was closed. If she did find a way to get inside, she'd be violating the law. Trespassing at the minimum. More likely, breaking and entering. Larceny. She had spent her adult life using the law as a hammer on those doctors and hospitals that took advantage of the sick and vulnerable. How could she blithely ignore that same code of law now? The law wasn't a *sometimes* covenant for her. The law needed to be consistently followed, not just when it was convenient. That was the beauty of it, one of the things that drew her to it in the first place, how it was black and white and well-defined.

Through the chain link fence, she could see rows of shrubs and pallets of bagged mulch. It was quiet. Deserted.

Janet moved in to get a closer look. She wasn't going much further without fuel, and she wasn't in any condition to walk the next couple hundred miles. She certainly wouldn't be trapped here in a store parking lot.

She noticed a pallet of bagged lawn fertilizer sitting against and just outside of the fence. After some consideration she climbed the bags, using them like a staircase to mount the fence and ease herself down the other side into the retail yard.

It was fortuitous that the bags were stacked there. In her weakened state, she would not have been able to scale the fence. As it was, she was winded and needed to pause to collect herself.

'If that's all it takes to get into the property, I'm surprised they have anything left here,' she thought to herself. She looked around, but

there was still no sign of anyone. The registers near the gate stood unattended. Only sparrows moved among the outdoor shelving. She continued to the side entrance that led from the outside retail yard into the store.

She shielded her eyes and pressed her face against the glass, peering into the gloom of the store. It seemed empty. *'Dead'* she thought grimly.

Janet mustered a soft and tentative "Hello?" She tested the large sliding glass doors. Her recent experience made her afraid to make too much noise and attract attention to herself.

She offered a few light, tentative raps on the glass with her knuckles, her wedding ring making a metal-on-glass *tack tack tack* sound. But it seemed obvious that there was no one there.

The power was down, so the automatic doors were going to be anything but automatic. These wouldn't be regular glass doors either. She knew that from her knowledge of liability laws. Tempered glass, and probably laminated. Hard to break.

She was at a turning point now. The only way in was to force or break the doors. She considered this. It was a bit of a Rubicon moment for her.

In the current situation, her hesitancy to break in might seem an anomaly, but respect for the rule of law was part of the fabric of her being. It was part of how she defined herself, and it was a bright line she had never crossed.

In normal times, to do so would be a betrayal of what she stood for and what she believed herself to be. Especially if what she had been through in the city was an anomaly, she was about to become no better than a looter in a riot.

She shook her head and decided it had to be done. *'I can plead necessity and even compensate them for the damage. They've certainly got bigger fish to fry,'* she justified.

Looking around for something to use to break the glass doors, she settled on a six-foot metal fence post. There were bundles of them stacked between two pallets of flowering roses. The tools of the door's destruction, and maybe hers, nestled between the sweet-smelling blooms. Sweet smelling or not, the posts were heavy and pointed and should be able to break a hole in the glass.

Hefting a fence post, she backtracked to a display by the registers and pulled on a thick pair of new work gloves. Her soft lawyer hands were not tough enough to take the punishment.

How to actually break the doors with the fence post took some figuring out. She first tried to pry them open using the metal fence post as a lever, but that wasn't going to work. She'd have to break out one of the glass panels on the door.

This was going to make some noise. But it had to be done. She didn't want to attract attention. '*Maybe if she was quick about it...*' she thought. There was a strong wind that would naturally mute the impact sounds. The tall brick walls of the back of the store would direct sound into the trees behind.

Backing up a few steps, she ran at the door like a medieval knight jousting. With each lunge, she'd stop and listen as the loud bangs echoed through the quiet yard and sent the sparrows flying in panic.

The reverberations shook up her hands and arms and rattled through her shoulders. She was glad to have put on the gloves or she probably would have torn the skin from her hands as the fence post twisted and pulled through her grip.

Each time, even as she took a beat to gather herself and listen, no one appeared. All she could hear was the wind in the treetops and the birds.

She began to develop a rhythm with her charges, and on the fifth one, the glass cracked. She carefully collapsed the laminate until she had enough space to crawl through, but not before grabbing a nearby push broom and sweeping the broken glass into a pile off to one side. *'No sense creating a liability problem'* she thought, instinctively. Even now, with mounting evidence to the contrary, Janet clung to the belief that a world with law and order existed.

***

The store was as dark as a crypt. Even at this end, with the light filtering in from the yard, the interior of the store quickly dissolved into a black void. She waited. Listening. There were small noises in the store. Rustling and cracking. It smelled of disinfectant and dust.

Janet inched forward as her eyes adjusted enough to make out the aisles.

She wished she had a flashlight. Then she remembered her phone and fished it out of the side pocket of her yoga pants. *'Yoga pants,'* she thought incredulously, and made a mental note to find some other clothes.

What would be good for roughing it? Jeans? Overalls? Probably not yoga pants.

'Yoga probably isn't on the agenda today…' she mused, still trying to transition mentally from the normal world of a couple of weeks ago to the reality now facing her.

She knew her phone was worthless as a phone, but she had kept it on the charging cable in the rover and could still use it as a flashlight. She couldn't help but look at it. "No network connection", the display said, with a red exclamation point.

'No nothing,' she thought ruefully.

Who would she call, anyway, if she had a signal? Who was left? Not Jim and the kids. They were dead in the apartment. She had to brace herself again as a wave of grief surged and receded.

Maybe her parents? That's where she was headed. A small town on the South Carolina side of the state line between Greenville and Asheville. That's where she grew up.

She'd find out in a couple of days—if she could just find some fuel.

The great blackness of the store swallowed the white circle of light projecting from her phone. She felt small in the darkness. As she moved forward, shapes appeared suddenly out of the gloom, like apparitions, only to resolve into lawnmowers and wheelbarrows. The fear of a lone human in an unknown, dark place, making machines into monsters.

She tripped over a sign and fell face-first onto the floor, dropping her phone in the process. Panicking, she scrambled to her feet and found the wayward device. She wanted to get out of here, but she needed those gas cans.

After a few passes through the aisles in the home landscaping section, she found them - the big, red five-gallon plastic containers with spouts that she had been looking for. "Score," she said quietly, as if not to awaken the monsters living in this dark place.

Next to finding some hose.

She had an inspiration and looked around the area of the gas cans with her light and was delighted to find one of those siphoning hoses with the big plastic bulb you squeezed to create the suction. That would save her from having to get a mouthful of diesel.

"Double score," she said, maybe a bit louder this time, as she was getting used to the darkness and the sound of her small voice echoing around the tall shelving.

It didn't look like anyone had been in the store since they closed it up. The products were still neatly stacked on shelves and hung on hooks. Like some sort of darkened shrine to suburban America.

Janet padded her way back to the outdoor section of the Garden Center with the cans and siphon hose and carefully lowered them over the fence.

Before climbing back over, she turned back to face the store. It seemed safe enough, quiet enough. She had already crossed the point of no return. She figured she might as well see what else she could find. She was already on the hook for larceny, what was the harm now? She argued with her better self that she would only take what was needed, nothing more.

As she moved back toward the store, she thought she might have heard a vehicle over the background thrum of the wind. She couldn't tell from what direction. Maybe the highway behind her. It was hard to tell now that the wind had picked up. Looking at the sky, it seemed like a storm might be approaching. There were dark clouds rolling up from the southwest.

Despite her wariness, she pushed through the portal of shattered glass once more. She thought the void looked just as dark and impenetrable as before, maybe more so with the approaching storm dimming the sunlight. But it somehow seemed less threatening the second time around. That's how fear worked, thriving mostly in the unknown.

Still, the long dark aisles seemed to press in on her, like the lid of a coffin. *'This would be a bad place to get caught,'* she thought. The aisles were designed to funnel traffic and maximize shelf area, but now they felt more like a series of box canyons to be trapped in.

She made her way through toys and electronics into the sporting goods section. She shined her light into a display case loaded with boxes of ammo. Another had some hunting knives. She thought better of breaking into it. She could argue the need for fuel, but what jury would sympathize with her breaking into a locked weapons display? That's something that a looter would do. That compounded the larceny.

She sighed and moved on.

"Let's see if there is any food or water left," she said out loud, but in a hoarse whisper. Surely the taking of food would be justified in this circumstance.

She was deep into the dark store now as she made her way to the farthest end – the grocery section.

Most of the water and food had been cleared from the shelves. Probably by panic buying in those few days when people knew what was happening but didn't know how bad it was going to get. Classic human behavior. Milk, bread, eggs, and toilet paper.

'A lot of good milk and bread are going to be to dead people,' she thought.

A couple of liters of water and some apple juice were all she could find. Better than nothing. In the next aisle, there were some cans of nuts and coconut milk. Good, calorie-dense food. Would last a while too. Finally, with an additional bag of chips clutched under one arm, she figured she should get back to the safety of the Range Rover.

Then she heard it.

A low rumbling from out in front of the store. She froze and listened as the sound grew louder and more distinct. Janet froze and focused as she heard it accelerate across the parking lot, heading for the store.

There was a terrific crunch as a pickup truck smashed into and through the front doors of the store.

She hit the floor and tensed.

There was the sound of truck doors opening as a man whooped in celebration. "Holy Crapoli! I told you it would work!" He sounded drunk.

"Yeah, it worked, but we're going to need a new truck."

"Don't worry, Hoss, there's thousands of new trucks out there! What color do you want?"

The other man laughed, "I'll take a bright orange one with the Stars and Stripes!"

"You got it, man. Ready to do some shoppin'?"

Janet frantically switched off the flashlight in her phone and groped her way back towards safety.

Who were these men? They made her breaking and entering look like child's play.

She needed to get out of there. Should she drop the goods she had scavenged to make a faster getaway? No, the men didn't know she was there, and dropping stuff would make more noise anyhow. She shifted her grip trying to keep the bag of chips from crinkling.

Her heart was racing, and she was breathing hard now. It took everything she had to suppress a cough as the heavy breathing brought phlegm up from her recovering lungs. Her eyes watered as she squeezed down the spasms.

The light from the Garden Center doors reflected yellowish in her eyes like a small window at the end of a long, dark hall. She stayed low, trying to be as quiet as she could. Through the cracked door, she pushed her haul and crawled out behind it. She made her way quickly through the yard to the fence. Carefully, she dropped her goods onto the fertilizer bags to deaden the impact, climbed over the fence, and made her way hurrying towards the dumpsters.

She gently eased the hatch of the Range Rover open and threw in her stash. She slid behind the wheel and closed the door softly. The quiet click of the door latch was like music to her ears as she was now back in her safe space, but she was not yet in the clear.

What to do next? They didn't know she was here. She could just hunker down in the car and wait for them to go. But that didn't feel right to her. She didn't like being in a corner and having to make defensive decisions. Reacting to others robbed her of the initiative. Her life had been one of being in charge and on the offensive.

She knew she didn't want to meet them. Clearly, they were out of control. All her equivocating around *her own* larcenous acts looked silly now. This was a full-on loss of control – looting and anarchy!

Janet gritted her teeth and turned the key in the ignition. The big diesel caught. It was quiet for a big car. Besides, they were inside the store, hopefully as inebriated as they sounded. They probably wouldn't even know she was ever here.

Gingerly, she rolled the car around toward the front and peeked around the corner. The ass-end of a pickup truck was sticking out where the front doors of the store should have been, broken glass and scattered inventory around it like grave goods.

She still needed fuel. The low-fuel light told her that she had ten to twenty miles of easy driving left before it would be critical. Hopefully, that truck was dead, because if they chased her, who knows how far she could get. Might have been a safer bet to hide behind the dumpsters than to deal with these yahoos in the middle of nowhere with the Range Rover dead.

But she was committed now.

Just then, one man came staggering out of the hole in the store where the truck was impaled. He tripped and fell to his knees and rose again, trying to run. A second man emerged behind him, holding what looked like a pistol.

She held her breath.

The man in pursuit was screaming. Some expletive-filled rant about who was the boss. Then he raised his arm, pointed at the back of his companion's head, and—shot. He shouted something else as the first man crumpled to the pavement.

In her horror, Janet stomped on the gas and made for the parking lot exit, instinctively ducking as though she expected bullets to come crashing lethally through the back window, like in the movies. But *nothing* came.

A quick glance back showed the man waving his gun arm at her in an almost befuddled way.

Was this the new world? Men behaving like animals? No consideration for laws or morality? Was it like this everywhere?

She had been worried about stealing some mixed nuts and this man just committed a murder as though it was nothing!

***

As the storm clouds gathering to the southwest darkened the road, the realization that what happened in the city wasn't a fluke settled into her psyche.

It wasn't just that the world and the people that she loved were dead.

This world was far from dead.

This world was dangerous.

Dangerous with the unbridled violence of the most insidious of beasts. She had beaten the disease, but now she had to deal with the sad remnants of humanity too.

She turned back onto the street and accelerated away into the darkening horizon.

This *was* a new world. She was going to have to face it. She was going to have to harden herself up. She was going to have to change her assumptions before *she* became the victim -

before *she* found herself face down in a parking lot with the full force of a bullet to the back of *her* head.

"No!" She shouted out loud, emphatically as the Range Rover vibrated, as if she were giving herself an order.

Janet Kramer was never the victim.

Chapter Seven - Bill the Dog

December 14th – Six weeks since the virus ended the world...

Bill the Dog watched the old man cooking over a low fire at the edge of a swamp.

It wasn't a fire that humans would likely see or smell, but a dog's nose was different. Bill had picked up the scent of cooking game and followed it.

It was an overcast winter day. The days were noticeably colder, especially at night. The leaves had blown from the trees.

Bill lay concealed in the underbrush. Silent. Watching. Curious.

The old man's dinner wasn't the only scent on the breeze. There was, as always, the background smell of smoke and death that seemed to permeate the apocalypse, but there was something else, too.

There was the smell of other dogs.

***

The old man squatted next to the small fire, cooking a rabbit he had snared. He kept the fire low to keep from attracting any unwanted attention from other survivors. He had spent enough time in the great outdoors to know how to build and manage a discreet cooking fire, and enough time in the apocalypse to know the value of discretion.

The place he had chosen was a low spot, off the road and sheltered. The ground where he built his fire was protected on one side by a large swamp. With his back against the swamp, he couldn't be surprised or flanked. No one was going to come from that direction easily without him knowing it.

At least, that was his plan. He was trying to be more cautious given his recent brushes with personal extinction, trying to use whatever knowledge and skill he possessed to avoid more of those interactions.

The old man mused about swamps and humans.

Most modern humans tended to avoid swamps, but that hadn't always been the case. Marshes and swamps could be powerful redoubts for those practicing the refugee lifestyle.

He thought of the Marsh Arabs living an isolated and protected life in the swamps of Mesopotamia for hundreds of years until eventually Saddam Hussein and the Iraqi government drove them out. Even then, they were forced to redirect the Euphrates and drain the marshes to get the Marsh Arabs to resettle.

Or famously, Alfred the Great, leading a successful campaign to retake Wessex and then all of England from the marsh Island of Athelney. The Norse had him on the ropes but couldn't finish him. They drove him into the swamp and left him for dead.

From that island in the swamp, Alfred had rallied the Anglo-Saxons of Somerset and Wessex to drive the Great Heathen Army out of England.

Or so went the tale.

All that from a swamp.

'Maybe over a thousand years ago Alfred squatted over a low fire, cooking game just like me,' the old man thought. He looked around, making sure he was still alone. There might not be marauding Norse, but there were pillagers in the apocalypse who would not hesitate to kill him for his food.

The old man sliced the cooking meat with his long knife. It sizzled a bit over the open flame.

Almost ready.

A noise made him start. The crunching of leaves or the breaking of sticks underfoot. He sensed it. Something stood out from the background noises of nature.

He was not alone.

The old man instinctively grabbed a piece of wood from his firewood pile. He scanned the tree line for the source of the disturbance and saw a dog crouching in the shadow of an oak tree.

"Hey boy!" The old man called out. "Whatcha doing?"

There were a lot of dogs wandering in the apocalypse, their masters having been felled by the disease; they now roamed this dead world looking to survive.

He had never had a dog. No room for it in the city. No room in the apartment and no room in their busy lives back then. In his subsequent life, after he'd lost his license and fled to Africa there certainly was no room for a dog and the complications it would bring.

He took care of himself. He didn't need the extra burden of some mutt in his life.

The old man wondered if dogs were susceptible to the virus. Probably not. At least not until it ran out of human hosts and mutated again.

The dog was a nondescript brownish mutt of some sort. Big jaws. Probably some pit bull in it. It stared at the old man and his fire but did not move from its crouch. Its eyes were locked on him, and it held like a statue.

He called to it again. "What's up, dog?" And brandished his length of firewood to show that he wasn't unprepared.

The old man probably wouldn't have noticed the second dog if it wasn't for his defensive position hard up against the edge of the swamp. This dog, the second one, was slowly moving in on him from the side. The old man recognized that these dogs were not here for belly rubs and a quick game of fetch.

He tensed and threw the piece of firewood at the second dog. It sidestepped and remained in a stalking crouch, undeterred. The old man looked around for something which he could ward them off. He grabbed a good-sized stick that lay nearby, rose, and turned to face this new visitor.

This one was bigger with a matted, mottled fur from roving too long outside in the weather. It growled low and angry. Its face and head were scarred with scabby gashes - tooth or claw marks from some recent fight.

The old man had experienced dog packs before in his travels. One dog wasn't typically a problem. Two or more dogs were a pack. And packs had a different psychology. Packs hunted. He'd seen this, or versions of it in his life. Canids would look to surround a man and attack. Once one could grab an arm or a leg, they would all pile on.

The unlucky victims of dog packs were torn to pieces bit by bit until they bled out or died from shock.

Two more dogs appeared from the edge of the brush and moved menacingly around him, trying to find the blind spot to attack. The old man picked up a handful of gravel and flung it at the leader, shouting and brandishing his stick threateningly.

The lead dog ignored the volley and lunged, growling.

The old man swung his stick at it.

Another made a lunge from behind. The old man spun and parried with the point of the stick. The dog grabbed and snapped at the offered stick, mindless and feral.

The old man was talking to himself as he backed down the bank into the swamp, "Keep them in front of you. Let them have the rabbit. Maybe they'll go away."

But the pack pursued him, step by step, heads low, bodies tensed to spring at any opening.

The animal madness of the pack.

They were above him on the bank now, spread out to get the best angles.

He backed down slowly into the marsh. Warm muddy water bathed his feet as he felt around for solid ground to stand on.

They kept coming. The pack was patient and mechanically intent. They would pursue until he made a mistake.

Step, by muddy step, the old man continued backing carefully into the swamp. Water and mud up to his knees, feeling the bottom with his feet.

The pack hesitated at the water's edge but then bounded in as one with splashing leaps. But the change in territory seemed to take some of the enthusiasm out of their pursuit. They picked their way through the mud carefully with eyes on the old man.

The old man looked around quickly. He couldn't indefinitely wade in the swamp. He needed to find a defensive position.

He continued to back across the muddy water, angling towards a sort of hummock or small lump island not more than a couple feet across, covered with tangled brush and a small tree. If he could just put his back against that tree, he might be able to hold them off.

Backing up onto the hummock, he slipped, and the lead dog lunged again. He managed to regain enough footing to brandish the stick and make it back off. The old man scooched with his elbows up onto the hummock and used the small tree to lever himself back into a standing crouch.

The dogs surrounded him and circled. There was a flash and a splash to his right, and he felt the pain in his leg as the dog bit. He screamed, "Motherfucker!" and brought the stick down violently on the dog's head and shoulders - hard enough for the stick to break. The dog yelped and released its hold.

The old man was starting to panic now. The adrenaline was coursing through his body and his heart was pounding. He may have growled himself.

They were on him close now, snapping at anything within reach. He swung the half-stick like a club, wildly back and forth, shouting and kicking.

"Get off me!" He screamed. "No!" And "Down!"

As he desperately cast about to survive, his inner narrative was considering that this might be the end, torn to pieces by a pack of feral dogs in a swamp. '*Good an end as any,*' he thought grimly, as resolve mixed with panic and surged through his body. These dogs were about to add him to the great pile of bones that was humanity's legacy.

Dogs... Bones... There was some sort of joke in there.

He was getting tired, and they knew it.

Breathing hard. Heart racing. Desperate. There were four of them.

He couldn't keep it up.

Just as he was threatening with one more weak swing of his makeshift club, the dogs froze, heads cocked in unison. That weird, still-picture moment that affects dogs when something enters their doggy radar.

The old man watched as a large, curly-haired dog bounded down the bank, out into the swamp. This was a big dog. Head and shoulders above the pack. He saw it coming and thought, *'Uh oh! Here come the reserves to clean up!'*

But the curly one didn't go for the old man. Instead, he exploded into the pack like a bowling ball into set pins. Like a whirling dervish. A blur of fur and teeth.

The pack was confused and lost cohesion as it was interrupted in its hunt by this party crasher.

The big curly newcomer isolated one of the smaller brown dogs with a leaping splash, pinned it down with its big paws, and tore into its face. The brown dog squealed away, breaking free with a bloody ear hanging loose.

The curly-haired dog turned to face the others with blood dripping from its bared teeth, ears pinned back, shoulder muscles twitching with anticipation, and began to advance.

The larger pack dog considered the option to fight, but apparently didn't like the odds. It slunk away with its allies towards dry land.

Backing out of the swamp the way they came, heads low and growling the whole way.

The big, curly-haired dog stood tall with its back towards the old man and watched the pack leave. He took one or two menacing steps and barked when they appeared to slow their retreat.

They got the message and kept going.

The big, curly-haired dog sat with a plop in the shallows and dropped its shaggy head to take a drink of muddy water. He stood again and shook the water from his coat. He turned to the old man with a cocked head and an *aww shucks* look. He kicked a few handfuls of muddy water with his back paws in disdain in the direction of the retreating feral curs.

The old man was slightly in shock and did not know how to take this new visitor.

This apparition.

What just happened?

The old man tentatively held out his shaking hand and said something dumb.

"Good boy...?"

It was all he could muster as the adrenaline drained from his brain.

The big, curly-haired dog cocked his head again and sniffed the offered hand. He wagged his peacock tail and advanced happily to lay his big head against the old man's thigh.

The old man cradled the big head in his shaking hands. "Good boy," he said again, with more conviction now. "Thanks for that. I appreciate the help." The big curly head nuzzled closer.

The old man tried to make sense of what happened. He was ready to die. This big dog had come to his rescue. It had been a close call. Could he trust this dog now? Did he have a choice? What the hell was going on anyhow? Every time he was ready to lay down and let the end come it didn't happen.

Why did this dog save him?

The old man lifted the big head in his hands while scratching behind the ears, inspecting this new protector. "We gotta get you some flea and tick meds, big guy. Maybe a hairbrush."

Looking suspiciously at the curly mane, the old man reconsidered. "Well, maybe not a hairbrush, but let's get out of this mud and see if we can save that rabbit."

Chapter Eight - Fork in the Road

The old man separated a leg from the cooked rabbit with his long blade and tossed it to the big dog.

Since they had crawled out of the swamp, the dog had been laying prone, like a sphynx, a few feet away, watching the old man.

The dog's large curly head rested on extended paws; his expressive brown eyes under bushy eyebrows watched intently, like he was weighing the old man, assessing him in that impenetrable doggie brain.

The dog sniffed at the proffered food and cocked an inquisitive glance at the old man, one eyebrow raised.

"Go ahead," the old man said, "It ain't filet mignon from a five-star, but it will keep you going."

The old man tore a bit off for himself and stuck it in his mouth, chewing hopefully.

"See? Yummy," the old man lied, making yummy noises and rubbing his belly in pantomime as he chewed the tough meat.

"Mmm...tastes like chicken!" he continued, winking at the dog.

The dog continued to look at him intently.

"It's the least I can do, after you probably saved my life. Go ahead, eat up. My treat."

The dog cocked its head.

"Don't worry. You can get the next one." The old man grinned.

The dog seemed to make a decision. It army-crawled forward and delicately took the rabbit leg into its mouth. Thoughtfully the dog held the bone down with his paws, pulled small pieces off, and swallowed them without much chewing.

"You are a strange one," the old man said to the dog. "Here you come, tearing into that pack like a berserker, but you eat like it's Sunday tea."

The old man wondered about the dog as they both ate in silence.

What was this dog's story? Where did he come from? The dog looked healthy enough. Seemed to be well cared for. Unlike those feral mutts that tried to tear him apart in the swamp.

The old man considered that the dog's owner might be nearby and, even though the dog didn't seem dangerous, the human might be.

He'd need to keep his head up and stay alert to the dog's body language.

Maybe the owner was dead, and the dog was left adrift in the apocalypse?

Did it really make any difference to the old man? This dying world was full of castoffs and vagabonds, unhinged from the old world, disconnected, and floating like trash in new, dark currents.

He gestured to the dog. "Live and let live, that's what I say."

Not that the old man had anything left to live for. His family was gone. Except for one son that hadn't been accounted for.

It was ironic. The old man had never been involved much in his kids' lives. That was his wife's job, he had thought. His job was to be a famous doctor.

It wasn't until he had lost everything that he had gotten to know his youngest son, Paul. It's funny how that works. They had come together at the end.

Paul had taken those first shaky steps with an olive branch across the family divide, fraught with tears and recrimination.

Now the old man felt he owed Paul this resolution.

That was the last thing on the old man's To Do list before he could crawl onto the big pile of bones and let it all go.

He was tired. He was done with this world. He had this one last thing to do. Then he was done. One thing he was sure of was that he didn't need a dog, and he didn't need any friends.

It was too late to build new bonds in this dead world. The old man breathed deeply and sighed. "To hell with it," he muttered, as if to put a period on the end of a summary paragraph. "Just keep moving."

He gnawed on the last bits of the rabbit until there was nothing but bones. He tossed them to the dog, stood up, and wiped his hands on his shorts.

"To hell with it."

He felt the bite on his ankle when he stood. It could have been much worse.

Annoying but nothing career-ending. The attacking dog had gotten mostly socks. Still, he would need to clean it before he moved on. It would be ironic to die of sepsis or flesh-eating bacteria from the swampy water now that he had survived the attack.

The old man put out the fire with some swamp water and began to collect his things. The dog was still sitting sphynx-like, watching him with one cocked eyebrow.

The man checked his pack and adjusted some things to make sure it wouldn't bounce too much or rub the wrong way. He didn't need any raw skin that could potentially lead to an infection.

He hoisted the pack onto his shoulders and shrugged it into place.

The dog stood up now too, with an alert bearing of anticipation, as if ready for some further action on the old man's part.

The old man reached down and scratched the curly head behind the ears. "OK, buddy. Thanks again for the help. I'm moving on now. Got one last thing to do. Heading west. Have a good life."

It was here that the old man noticed, for the first time, the big dog was wearing a collar. A black nylon affair with a couple of tags on it that jangled a bit when he scratched under the dog's chin.

He knelt on one knee, eye level with the dog. "Let's see what we got here?"

The dog didn't react and let him look, head raised and placid.

One of the tags was a rabies tag.

"Good to know you're up to date on your vaccinations, buddy."

The next tag was something that you might make in one of those penny arcade machines. It had an ornate "B" on it surrounded by a sort of star or wreath etching.

The old man considered this.

"OK, 'B' ... I gotta go. Been a slice of heaven. You stay safe."

With this the old man began trotting down the dirt road, heading west.

He fell into his easy trot and looked up at the sky. The weather looked clear and there were a few more hours of sun. He should be able to get another ten miles or so today.

The weather had been getting colder at night. He'd need to find some long pants and a winter jacket, maybe even a sleeping bag, although he hated to carry too much stuff. It still got cold in the winter down here in the south at night, especially inland. He knew the weather could turn fast in these parts and freezing to death would be just too ironic to let happen.

Lost in thought, the old man still couldn't help but notice the rhythmic drumbeat of the dog's trot behind him.

The dog fell in behind him for a few paces and then moved out ahead like a picket. It took a position about three yards out and paced the old man, scanning ahead and pausing to look back every once in a while.

"OK, B. It's a free country. I can't stop you from running down this road with me, but I don't need a dog!" The old man hissed defiantly in the dog's direction.

The dog did not respond.

Feeling the matter of not needing companionship resolved, the old man settled back into his trot.

"You're a decent runner, B. That's a good skill to have in the apocalypse. What does the B stand for, anyway? Bart?"

The dog did not respond.

"Bob?"

More silence.

"Umm... Buddy? Boxcar Willie? Ben? Blake? Brad?" No response from the dog.

What *would* you call a dog like this? He was a biggish dog. Some sort of wolf-hound mix, maybe? He had a large head, short curly hair, and a feathery tail with a bit of an insouciant kink upwards that gave an impression of dandiness when he trotted.

He was obviously a good athlete. Not bouncy or frenetic like a sheepdog, but strong, reserved, and powerful when he needed to be.

"I know!" The old man smiled, warming to his game, and secretly glad for the company. "You're one of those pampered dogs, with a gold dog bowl and ribbons in your hair at the country club...and your name is... Baby!" The old man drawled out the syllables mockingly, "*baaay-beeee"*.

Still no response. They trotted along in silence - the old man lost in thought. What was the name of that guy in California he knew? The surfer?

"Bill?" The old man blurted, as the memory popped out from the dust of his brain.

The dog's ears perked up and he turned to look at the man.

"Bill," he repeated, testing.

The dog responded with a look that said, plain as day, '*What*?'

"Well, Bill the Dog, it's a pleasure to make your acquaintance."

They continued to trot down the dirt road west, man and dog. Man talking and telling stories. Dog listening and staying alert for danger.

After a while, the old man started to worry. *What was he doing?* This dog seemed to want to hang around. It wasn't that he didn't *like* dogs; he did. That wasn't the point. He even liked this dog more than most - the dog had probably saved his life.

The question was, did he really need a dog in his life right now? And how would he take care of a dog anyhow? How would he keep this big boy fed? Could this dog even keep up with him? Would it bark and attract attention at the worst possible moment and get him killed?

The bottom line here was that the old man wasn't looking for any new friends in the apocalypse. *'Friends'* caused bad decisions and got you killed. He'd spent years retreating from the company of man. He had acquaintances. He had trail buddies. He didn't have friends.

The old man stopped running. He scowled at the dog as these considerations raced through his mind. The dog, as if sensing his indecision, leaned his big head against the old man's hip and looked up at him.

"Jeezus..." the old man said, putting his hand on his new acquaintance's head. "You're something, aren't you? OK, let's go Bill."

About twenty minutes into the run, there was a fork in the road and the old man chose the road on the right because it seemed to point more west according to the position of the sun.

Bill the Dog quickly flanked out in front of the old man, blocking his way and barking.

"Listen dog, I'm going this way. If you want to come, fine. But get out of my way."

Bill the Dog would have none of it.

Even when the old man tried to go around, Bill would move to block, barking and barring the way.

The old man stopped to consider this. What was with this crazy dog? Already being loud and getting in the way. What did it want? Did it know something he didn't? He had to consider the fact that this dog had already saved his life once.

As the old man thought and took a drink, Bill the Dog took a few steps down the other fork and circled, looking at the old man and barking.

"Really, Bill?" The old man asked. "I get it, you want me to go that way. But shouldn't the human with the big prefrontal cortex be making these kinds of decisions for himself?"

But behind his bluster and ego, the old man considered that the dog might be warning him of something. Some danger the old man could not see but the dog could? Did it really matter anyhow?

The old man resigned himself to the dog's directions. "OK, Bill. I'll play along this time but don't think it sets a precedent. Either of these roads are heading west-ish." And with a sigh, he acquiesced. "Let's go."

Bill trotted ahead, with a bit more urgency now, looking back over his shoulder at the old man occasionally to make sure he was keeping up.

The old man scanned the tree line, with some alertness himself, wondering what had gotten into this dog. Why was it acting agitated?

It wasn't more than a couple hundred yards more down the dirt road that a low ranch house came into view.

The house was set back in the trees. A short gravel driveway led to the side where there was a van with handicapped plates parked under a corrugated metal awning. There was a ramp, that seemed to be a more recent addition, leading from the driveway to the front porch and the door.

Bill stopped and his body language made it clear that this was where he had been leading the old man.

Chapter Nine - Home Again

November 27th – Fourth week since the virus ended the world...

The skies were darkening as Janet eased the Range Rover onto the entrance ramp to the expressway. Her hands trembled as she gripped the steering wheel hard, adrenaline still pumping through her body.

"That man just committed murder right in front of me," she said, not sure if she could believe it. What the hell was going on? What was this nightmare? Was it like this everywhere?

"Focus, Janet!" she barked out loud like a drill sergeant, mentally slapping herself. "You have to find some diesel and get to where you're going." She had to hold it together. She was the one who *always* held everything together when everyone else was panicking.

Janet thought of her parents. It was about a thousand miles from New York City to where they lived. She had driven it before. It was a long day. The trip took fourteen or fifteen hours of driving if she pushed through and didn't stop too much. Maybe more if there was traffic and construction.

When she had made this trip with the kids, they did it in two days, stopping midway to sleep in a hotel. *'Oh my God! The kids!'* she thought as a wave of melancholy rose up. She pushed it aside and focused on the empty highway flashing towards her.

She had to get to her parents. It would be safe there. She just had to push through and get there. What happened in the city, even those looters at the store, were anomalies. There were always anomalies in a crisis. *Disasters bring out the best and worst in people*.

'Focus Janet,' she thought, *'You're not thinking straight. Just get there and it will be ok.'* She nervously glanced and the 'low fuel' indicator.

She bore down for several long miles to the next exit where she saw a strip of small businesses. She pulled around back and found what she was looking for, a handful of large delivery vans parked in a row behind some sort of carpet installation business.

The wind was really picking up now and she could smell the rain, thick in the air with a hint of acrid smoke.

She'd have to hurry to beat the rain. To be safe, she made sure to position the car behind the one van that sat beneath the cover of a rusty awning. "Let's see what we can find," she told her over-tired self, pulling the cans and siphon hose from the back of the Range Rover.

After snaking the hose into the van's tank, Janet was able to get the siphon started with little trouble. She was glad this had not proved difficult and hoped to finish before the downpour. She was able to siphon enough to fill the Range Rover's tank.

Janet paused to sniff at the fuel vapors and observe the color of the stream exiting the hose. It was Deisel, not regular gasoline. Putting regular gas in the Rover would be a critical mistake. Even in her exhausted state, she knew better than to foul the Range Rover's engine and get stranded on the highway with a dead vehicle.

As she hurried to add a few more gallons to the plastic cans for reserve, the first large drops began to splatter loudly on the metal roof above. She topped off the final can, secured the cap, and turned to load the car – but not before the heavy stuff came.

And it came.

Janet stood under the safety of the awning as the heavens opened up and the rain fell in torrents. As she took in the full force of the downpour, a wave of exhaustion hit and overwhelmed her. It had been a nightmare of a day, filled with physical and psychological trauma. She had been knocked out of balance and her hard-fought for reality had been smashed.

Janet stood there, now wallowing in the rubble of that destruction.

The *deaths*. The *driving*. The *store*. The *murderous looters*... and the sickness still haunting her body. She'd need to be careful. Especially with her penchant for pushing herself too hard, she could push herself over the edge.

She may have already.

Janet Kramer, known as "KJ" to some, and "The Killer" to those unlucky enough to face her in court, was losing her mental battle with reality.

She wanted to push on through the night to her parents' home, the house she grew up in, but thought better of it. Some of the old Janet was there, to manage the frayed emotions, and think rationally.

She had to sleep. She wasn't sure if she could sleep, but she'd have to try.

Janet took advantage of a lull in the downpour and hurried to load the cans in the back of the car. She made her way around to the driver's seat. She drove through the strip of parking lots behind the businesses and eased the big car into a secluded spot that promised relative safety.

Janet locked the doors and wearily crawled her way into the back seats. She unbuckled her youngest's car seat, still there, from that other life before this nightmare began. She willed herself to move past the emotions that welled up inside her.

Her rational mind was telling her she didn't need it anymore, but it felt like it weighed a thousand pounds as she lifted it into the back. A few stale Cheerios and gummy bears scattered as she set it down. The moment lingered with her and brought a new layer of exhaustion as she laid down and gave herself up to the soft leather seats.

The storm raged outside. Gusts of wind and rain rocked the big car, as Janet, an exhausted shell of the woman she had been just a few weeks earlier, pulled her sweatshirt hood tight and drifted off into a fitful sleep.

This was not the deep sleep of peaceful exhaustion. It was a sleep punctuated with frantic dreams mixed with flashes of memories.

In some of these dreams, she was being chased and couldn't run because her legs wouldn't move. Or she would have a gun, but the bullets wouldn't fit. She woke trying to scream but her voice would not come.

As she lay there, sweating and distressed from a particular nightmare, she thought of how she had ended up in the city, as the corporate killer. It seemed like so long ago. Like a dream itself. Like it happened to someone else.

How *did* a small-town girl end up taking down Fortune 500 Med Tech companies?

Janet had always been bright, had always been driven, but there are hundreds of bright, driven girls in rural communities who end up as waitresses at the local truck stop. How did *she* break out? What made her different?

It was hardly a mystery...

Janet was given purpose and focus after the unthinkingly brutal mistakes made by the medical system resulting in the death of her sister during childbirth. "Failure to recognize distress" was how they phrased it. She had seen how the doctors and lawyers covered their tracks, and no one was held accountable.

Her path was set then. A switch flipped. Her unique ability to *focus* and *finish* turned on in response.

However, *purpose* alone still doesn't get a bright, focused, hardworking young woman into a big-city firm.

The final piece fell into place at a legal conference in Charlotte where she was presenting a mock trial as part of a student group. In that audience was the groundbreaking prosecutor and federal judge Deborah Blinkel.

Deb had recognized the talent, and maybe saw a little bit of herself in this ambitious, hard youngster. The judge took Janet under her wing and set her on a path that led to the scholarship and the placement.

Janet had done the rest. With uncanny ability and ambition, she had molded herself into the most feared attorney in the medical malpractice and fraud partnership.

She made more money than her parents had ever seen and was known in the industry as a rising star.

Janet wondered where her old mentor was now. She thought about the last decade of single-minded focus. Was any of it worth it?

But none of those hard-won career accomplishments had helped her save her family when the plague hit the city.

What was she going to do now? How would she recover from this blow?

Janet tried to forget the memories and fitful dreams. She refocused on trying to sleep - to have the energy to drive the remaining few hundred miles to her childhood home. To return to the place she had left a decade ago, left with dreams of slaying corporate dragons.

To go home...

***

The storm had passed when Janet finally gave up trying to sleep in the morning. It was starting to get light. A mourning dove was lamenting the new day with its plaintive calls. The air was filled with that wet dirt smell that reminded her of her childhood in the yard of her parents' home when a storm had passed. The last of the clouds were rolling by and the sun was trying to break through.

She hadn't slept much, but she had slept enough to survive, enough to drive on.

Even though she felt physically stronger, mentally, she was still in a dark place. Janet felt like the last days had been filled with one dreadful assault after another. Each new day was a further blow to her reality, tearing away at her battered core self, layer by layer.

Janet rinsed out her mouth with water, wishing she had stolen a toothbrush and some toothpaste in the store.

She thought of the day ahead, and knew she had both enough fuel and enough energy to get to her folks' house now. She eased the Range Rover back onto the highway for a few more exits.

Where she was going, there was no interstate highway. She'd need to get off onto one of the state roads.

She found what she was looking for, state highway 347, the numbers in a white shield on a black background. One of the innumerable two-lane blacktop highways that snaked from the center of one small town to the next.

These were the roads people used before the interstates were built. She didn't need the GPS on her phone to tell her that in a hundred miles or so she'd get to Rutney Village, where her mom and dad lived in their simple country home.

It was a pretty country. The farms, the long unbroken sections of woods. The state road hugged around the foothills of Appalachia. She could almost feel normal again. Almost breathe again.

She passed through small towns where the speed limit dropped suddenly from fifty to thirty miles per hour. She found herself slowing down out of habit, even before seeing the sign. The burned in memory of local speed traps looking to boost the county revenues. Memories of a self-important county-mounty or deputy moseying up to the car and saying something like *"We don't allow that kind of driving here, Ma'am"*.

Had the plague reached these parts? Would those local cops even still be alive? Wouldn't they be busy trying to shore up what was left of the local government? Or would they be hiding out with their families trying to survive? They probably wouldn't be lurking behind a billboard at the bottom of a hill on the highway into town waiting for cars with out-of-state plates to speed by.

In most of these small towns in America, the storefronts were vacant or reduced to nail salons and dusty second-hand shops. The idyllic small towns of the 1950s and 1960s were nothing more than shells cored out by Walmart and globalization. She once heard them described as "bomb craters" by some writer in the city.

Janet came upon a town now that was particularly post-card-pretty as she rolled through. It could have been any of a thousand similar small towns scattered across the backroads of America. Civic pride beamed from the brick-faced buildings and old oak trees guarded neat sidewalks at regular intervals. Like something snatched from a 1960s movie backdrop.

This town seemed to still have some of its old enthusiasm about it. She passed the well-maintained fire station and a large, clean-looking Baptist church. As if on cue the local courthouse came into view, bringing a wave of nostalgia. The Corinthian columns, like some squat temple snatched from Athens, plopped here to bring civilization to these aspiring citizens.

A bronze soldier rode an energetic, rearing horse on a granite plinth, frozen in time, celebrating some forgotten victory of great men.

The nostalgia was comforting in a way. Janet noticed she was breathing easier. The weight was lifting. Why had she ever left this beautiful, peaceful corner of the world for the city?

She caught movement out of the corner of her eye. Time slowed. She saw the brick as if in slow motion cartwheel slowly through the air and skip once off the hood. Then, as if someone had turned the speed back up there was a flash, the safety glass of the windshield spiderwebbed. An explosion of glass splinters covered the inside of the car.

Instantly filled with shock and fear she unconsciously swerved hard to the right and accelerated as a shotgun blast boomed close to the side and tore into the window behind her.

A blurred image of figures with hats and guns crouching behind the parked cars zoomed by, barely registering as she struggled to react.

Partly on purpose, and partly in panic, she swerved off the pavement and over the curb up onto the courthouse yard. There was shouting and another shotgun blast peppered the Range Rover. "Jesus!" she ducked and pulled the wheel hard.

The Range Rover skidded sideways, churning up the well-maintained turf of the courthouse yard and rocking up on two wheels as she fought to bring the big car back under control.

She managed to wrench the car out of its slide but not before sideswiping the granite plinth. There was a terrible scraping noise, and the war monument teetered, breaking at the horse's legs, not quite all the way through but enough to leave it dangling, bent, and deformed.

The Range Rover gained traction and shot out the other side of the yard, through a fence. The big car bounced back onto the pavement and Janet accelerated, weaving down Main Street and out of town.

She was breathing hard and checking to see if she was hurt. There was glass everywhere and some indicator lights were red on the control panel, but she seemed to be OK.

What just happened? All she saw was men in hats leaning across the hood of a parked car with shotguns. What were they trying to do? Did they think she was a threat?

'What the hell is going on?' she thought, brushing shards of safety glass out of her lap. Even out here in the peaceful small towns, there was murder and chaos. She wasn't sure how much more she could take – and she was

starting to worry about her parents, and what she might find...

The Range Rover was still running but had sustained some damage. There was the smell of steam from the engine and a noticeable shimmy in one of the front wheels. But she wouldn't stop. There wasn't that much farther to go, and she couldn't risk running into more trouble.

She kept moving. Thirty more worrisome miles on progressively smaller roads brought Janet to where she grew up. The familiar trees and stone walls filled her memories. Up ahead the large red mailbox with an American flag motif marked the entrance to her driveway.

As she pulled into the familiar, long, gravel driveway she saw the tailgate of a vehicle sticking out of the bushes. Approaching slowly, she realized that it was her father's Ram truck nose-down in the drainage ditch that ran alongside.

"Oh my God!" Janet gasped.

Chapter Ten - West

Janet stopped the Range Rover and threw it into park. The big car had apparently taken enough abuse and refused to keep running. The engine choked and coughed to a rattling halt.

Stepping out and quickly shaking the last of the glass fragments from her hair and clothes, she looked to see what was going on with her father's truck. It didn't look like it had crashed, more like it had simply rolled there. What had happened? She couldn't see any overt signs of trouble.

It was with a sense of dread that she climbed down into the ditch to check. She could make out a person inside through the back window.

She was afraid of what she would find. What horrible new discovery?

She thought about her dad's heart condition and hoped the stress of these times had not stricken him.

Bracing herself against the side of the ditch she reached to grab the handle of the truck door. She pulled the door open with a rusty squeak and found her father was there. He was slumped forward into the dashboard. The keys were still in the ignition and the radio was emitting an empty static hiss.

"Dad!?"

Frantically, she reached for him. She grabbed the loose denim of his jacket with one hand while bracing against the door frame with the other and pulled him away from the dashboard.

But he was gone...

He looked old and small. He was barefoot in jeans and a dirty white T-shirt under the denim jacket. She struggled to pull his lifeless body back into the seat, his grey beard matted with blood and phlegm.

Janet collapsed back into the weedy ditch and breathed for a moment, exhausted again and in shock.

What the hell was happening?

He had been a strong man, he had been strong for her, but the plague was stronger.

Another rock in her life gone. Another light put out. More death. This world continued to take from her. Was trying to break her.

With an abrupt realization, she thought of her mom.

She pushed the door to the Ram closed and climbed the weedy bank back to the Range Rover leaving her father's body in the truck. Janet leaned on her car and noticed the buckshot holes and a nasty scar along the side from its collision with the statue back in town. A hiss and a cloud of steam rose steadily from under the hood.

The Range Rover was beaten and broken. Another comforting fixture in her life being taken from her.

She had a moment of hesitation. The comfort and security of the big car held her like a warm, familiar hand. But now she needed to walk the rest of the driveway to the house. Janet left the car and locked it. Partly out of habit, and partly to protect her hard-won supplies.

She stumbled towards the house along the gravel drive that was hedged by junipers and smelled of decaying mulch. Her head was swimming from the physical exhaustion, the shock of finding her father's body, and the expectant terror of what was waiting for her in the house.

The long driveway telescoped in front of her.

But she felt herself being inexorably pulled now towards that familiar faded blue door. That familiar house. The house of her youth. White clapboard. Shingled roof.

With each unsteady step, the fear and apprehension grew. What would she find?

Janet pulled the broken screen door open and entered the house. She didn't see anything immediately out of place. There were no lights on, and it smelled almost the way she remembered. A sweet mélange of cedar, mothballs, and fifty years of her mother's cooking. Yet something else, something sour was in the air as well.

The dark paneling of the living room made it feel small and close. A worn and familiar leather couch was set in front of an old console TV, just as it had always been. A homemade quilt was folded neatly on the cushions with a commemorative pillow from a long-ago vacation trip.

Old Popular Mechanics and Better Homes and Garden magazine issues lay in a tarnished brass magazine stand with a folded copy of the local newspaper.

She heard a noise from the back of the house.

She braced a hand against the wall and walked down the long hallway towards her parents' bedroom. The dark paneling was cool and smooth as she slid her hand along, leaning for balance. As she made her way, the hall seemed to run at a canted angle in front of her like a funhouse effect.

Past the bathroom with its pale blue tile, past her old bedroom, and finally to the entrance to her parents' room.

Janet pushed the door open and saw her mother lying flat on her back in the bed beneath the blankets.

Was she alive?

The room was exactly as Janet remembered. The old, patterned wallpaper ran in regular vertical stripes down to the chipped baseboard. Heavy furniture and the broad dark wooden bed frame. A cross hung on the wall above.

Janet paused to take in the scene and took a breath expecting the slightly sweet smell of potpourri that she remembered and gagged. Everything was the same, except for the acrid, organic smell of sickness. The smell, a mixture of vomit and feces assaulted her.

Janet fell forward into the room towards the bed.

The old woman was alive, but very sick with the disease, struggling to breathe.

A shaft of sunlight spilled through the partially closed blinds and silhouetted her mother's face - pale, old, and wan.

The old woman moaned, and a chill wracked her small body. A droplet of blood trailed from one eye to the yellowing pillowcase. A convulsive fit of coughing and choking produced a bloody foam.

Janet was startled when her mother's eyes blinked open and the old woman smiled weakly. The smile was macabre with crusts of blood, like a Halloween parody version of her mother's smile.

"Mom…" Janet said softly.

"Jane…" Her mom whispered in return, "I knew …you'd come."

"Don't try to talk now, Mom. Hold on. I'll get you some water."

"No… Darling… Stay…. Let me look at you," Her mother appealed through struggling breaths.

Janet looked down at the frail old woman that was her mom and smiled. She sat next to the bed, reached out and took her mother's warm hand in both of her own, and lifted it to her cheek.

"I'm here, Mom. I'm here."

"Jane...your father...he went for help..." Her mother croaked.

Janet thought for a moment then looked away, shaking her head slowly. "I know Mom. It'll be ok."

A worried look passed her mother's ravaged face. "Where are the children? Are the children with you? Are they ok?"

Janet's hands shook noticeably, and her voice cracked. "They're ok Mom, everything is ok."

Her mother closed her eyes, and a bloody tear ran down her face.

"Jane, hand me my Bible..."

Janet picked up the well-worn leather-bound *word of God* from the end table and placed it into her mother's warm embrace.

***

Time seemed to slow down for Janet as she held vigil at her sick mother's bedside. She dozed as the adrenaline drained from her body and the intensity of the day's events passed through her in a wave of drowsiness.

When she roused, her mom was asleep, breathing those shallow rattling breaths. Janet went and poured a cold glass of water and brought it to the bedside table. She wetted a towel in the bathroom.

Her mother was unconscious.

Janet carefully pulled the soiled bedclothes off the old bed, gently shifting her mother's frail form and cleaning as best she could. She stashed the soiled linens in the washing machine in the laundry room off the pantry and tucked fresh sheets and blankets under and around the old woman.

She processed the cleaning robotically. She was all cried out. She was numb. She felt empty and directionless.

Her mother's eyes flickered open again as Janet wiped the cool, wet towel across her face.

"Jane," she whispered.

"I'm here, Mom. I'm going to take care of you. Just let me take care of you now. Everything is going to be OK now."

Her mother's look turned serious. "Jane, you know you're the best of us...the best part of us...you know that."

"I know, Mom."

"Jane, I've been talking to God."

Janet tried to smile reassuringly.

"It's OK now. He said it's OK. He said it's OK, Jane. I love you, baby Jane...He said it's OK."

"I know, Mom, just rest," Janet said, as tears welled again and began to spill down both cheeks. She laid her head next to her mother on the bed and gently rested her mother's hand on her wet cheek.

***

Janet lay that way long into the night. Even after her mother had drawn her last labored breath. The old woman had not passed easily. The disease raging through her frail body had caused great distress in the process. In the end, it was as much a release from suffering as a death.

Her mom was gone, her dad was gone, her family was gone; it was all gone now.

Everything. Everyone. All gone. What did she have left? Nothing.

***

The rest of the day she moved like a zombie, burying the earthly remains of her parents in a shallow grave, working the shovel like an automaton.

She wasn't hungry and didn't notice the thirst, but she forced herself to eat from her parents' larder to keep going. But to keep going for what reason she couldn't think.

She laid the withered remains of her mother, shrouded in a homemade quilt, next to her father.

She leaned on the shovel for support, looked down, and wiped the wet dirt off her blistered hands. What would she do now? What could she do? Everything was gone. She was wrung out. She had nothing left to give and nothing left to live for.

She was weak from her recent bout with the killing virus. Her muscles tremored, overtaxed from the effort of burying her parents. She felt the nausea of overexertion. She'd need to rest and recharge now.

Janet, loving daughter, mother, wife, who was also the hard-ass killer lawyer who never rested, who never lost, was being pounded into the ground like a broken stake.

She thought for a moment that she might just as well lay down in that grave with her parents. Why couldn't the disease have taken her too?

Janet picked up her mother's Bible and it flipped open to a section that had been held by an ornate bookmark with a picture of a saint. The banner beneath a woman in medieval garb read *Saint Agnes of Rome.*

Janet read the marked passage out loud in an exhausted whisper.

"Isaiah 43:5...

Fear not, for I am with you,

I will bring your offspring from the East,

And from the West, I will gather you."

"West," she repeated, as the words from the verse swirled in her head.

As she stood there, she heard gunshots and an explosion from the direction of the town. Black smoke rose over the tree line.

She had to keep moving.

Not because she had anywhere to go.

Not because of any purpose.

But because there was simply nothing left for her here.

Nothing but ghosts – and she didn't have the energy to talk to ghosts anymore.

Janet closed the old Bible, bent down, and tucked it into the quilt.

She picked up the shovel and covered the last connection to her old life with dirt.

***

Janet took a cold shower. The heater was out but there was still water pressure enough. She pulled on some of her old hiking clothes that her parents had stored in the attic. She marveled at how they still fit. Even with the weight loss of the past couple of weeks, she retained that fitness and leanness that she had as a star athlete on the volleyball team in high school and college.

She selected some jeans, a thick shirt, and a down vest along with a backpack.

She would keep moving but how? The Range Rover was dead. It had joined the corpses that littered her new world.

What should she do now?

She didn't feel like she could stay here. It held too many memories and too much emotion. What if those men from the city followed her? Sooner or later some survivors would come here and despoil this place. Her childhood home.

She felt like if she stayed here, she would die, one way or another. Whether from marauders or sadness.

No, it wasn't in her nature to hunker down and take on a bunker mentality. She was a kinetic creature. She needed motion.

She could rest. Maybe a day or two. Gather what she could of her supplies and then keep moving.

That was her best chance of survival.

Should she try to fix a vehicle? Maybe try to free her father's truck from the ditch? No, even if she could find a way to get it out, she couldn't bear the thought of living with the memory of his death.

After the chaos of the past few weeks, she didn't like the thought of being constrained by the limitations of roads and machines. She was fit enough to make her way overland. That would give her flexibility and options.

She'd move west on foot.

She tried to find her old hiking boots, but they were rotted out from sitting these years in the wet basement. She opted instead for an old pair of running shoes from college. They'd have to do.

She threw a sleeping bag and some food into the pack along with some pictures of her family and parents and started walking.

Janet slumped her way into the dirt trails and hills behind her house, heading vaguely west into the nothingness of forested hills.

She walked alone.

Eventually, when the exhaustion overcame her and the sun was low, she sat down on a tree that had toppled onto the road during the storm.

She put her head in her hands and breathed.

Emotions came at her in a rush. The loss. The death. The brokenness. It all swam into her mind, and she began to sob.

Her shoulders slumped and heaved as she was racked with sobbing - for her family, for her kids, for her husband – for everything she had lost and everything she had weathered in the last few days.

"You alright, miss?" A sudden voice shocked her out of her tears.

Janet, startled, looked over her shoulder to see a smiling man standing behind her. He was probably thirty five, with a bit of a beer gut and a trucker hat. He had a deer rifle slung on his back and a small camouflage duffle.

The man came closer.

"Can I help you, darlin'? These are strange times," he continued. "Ought not to be alone out here. What's your name?"

Janet turned her head and appraised the man with a sideways glance. He was smiling but his eyes were shifting around between her and the road and the woods.

Janet did not answer. She watched the man's body language and saw it turn from friendly to patriarchal.

"Another asshole predator," she thought.

But did it even matter? At this point with nothing left, was it even worth fighting? All those years she spent fighting and everything was gone anyhow.

"Just leave me alone." Janet finally said flatly.

"Well, I don't think I should," the man said, reaching out and putting his hand on her shoulder. "It ain't safe for a woman like you to be alone in these times."

Janet fought the urge to tense up at his touch. Instead, she relaxed and feigned resignation.

But something, something deep inside her lit like a small fire. She may have been broken, but she wouldn't acquiesce to a man like this while she still had breath in her body.

"You and me, we're going to be friends now..." He drawled.

As he leaned over her from behind, touching her, something inside her snapped.

She remembered those Krav Maga training sessions in the city. *Hit the soft points. Use improvised weapons.* The instructor had taught.

Like the uncoiling of spring, she brought the hard point of her elbow up into the man's throat in one, hard fast strike.

He staggered back with a shocked look on his face and tried to unsling his rifle. But she was on him, bringing a fist full of sand and gravel into his eyes.

"Stop!" He screamed, swinging blindly with his fists.

Janet, on her feet, circled out of reach. She grabbed a rock from the ground and threw it with the fury of a thousand souls at the man's head. He screamed and dropped to his knees.

The man was on the ground, curled up, holding his head. Janet kicked him a couple of times, spending her remaining fury in the act.

"Stay down!" she commanded.

She tossed the man's pack and rifle aside, out of reach.

She kicked him again for good measure.

Janet knelt on one knee and leaned in close. Staring coldly into his bruised and bloody face, she said "KJ, my name is KJ."

The man lay in the fetal position in the dirt blubbering blood and snot into his weeks-old neck beard. He clutched his hands and arms over his head for protection.

Janet straightened up to her full height and inhaled deeply.

If this was the way the world wanted to play it, so be it. In fact, *bring it on!*

She had nothing left to lose but she also had the skills to survive. She was uniquely suited for this new world.

Janet had spent the last fifteen years juggling work, life, and family. Now she only had to worry about one thing - survival. The world had turned against her. She owed it nothing.

That simplified things.

She gathered the man's pack and rifle. She'd take what she needed and make sure he didn't follow her to take potshots when she wasn't looking.

She left the man to his misery and headed west into the low sun. She was tired, but she had a new strength.

Renewed somehow. She built a wall between herself and those things, those people that had been taken from her. She was the killer now. And the killer would protect her.

Chapter Eleven - No Friends in the Apocalypse

December 14th - Six weeks since the virus ended the world...

The old man slowed to a walk as they approached the house where Bill was leading him. Were there people inside? Survivors? He wanted nothing to do with other humans right now. His experience had not been great with what was left of *them* in the apocalypse so far.

Bill the Dog, however, was growing more agitated and excited as they got closer.

The old man wasn't sure about this. He hadn't wanted a new friend, and he didn't like the idea of being led into trouble by a dog he had just met. Was this some sort of weird trap?

"Hey Bill," the old man called to get the dog's attention. "'Not for nothin', but I'm not sure about this."

The old man reached over his shoulder for the crossbow. Bill gave him a concerned look.

The house was a small, ranch-style house with moss on its roof shingles. In the dirt driveway, there was a van parked under a metal awning that slanted down from the house.

The house didn't look particularly well-kept or even lived in.

There was a long wooden handicap access ramp with two-by-four railings that wrapped up to a farmer's porch along the front. Like something added recently as an afterthought.

The old man approached cautiously.

Bill the Dog led the way, head low.

The old man made his way up the ramp to the porch and the front door. He cautiously knocked on the door frame.

"Hello, anybody in there?" And, looking back at Bill, added, "I brought your dog."

There was no response.

Bill the Dog pushed the old man out of the way and grabbed a knotted rope that hung from the door handle in his mouth.

The old man watched as Bill pulled the outer storm door open, then jumped up and landed with some force on the inner door which was ajar. It popped it open.

Bill disappeared into the house.

The old man hesitated on the threshold. "OK, Bill, I guess you live here."

The old man entered cautiously behind the dog. He readied his crossbow and held it low but ready.

It was an open floor plan with an old couch in a big living room area. There was a small wood-burning stove with a stack of split wood, but no heat came from it.

An American flag hung on the opposite wall. A framed picture of a young soldier was on the side table.

As his eyes adjusted to the dim lighting, the old man could see a figure in a wheelchair by the sink in the kitchen area.

Bill was at the chair licking a dangling hand.

"Mister...you okay?" The old man asked tentatively. "I'm sorry to come in, but the dog... Bill...he kinda led me here and opened the door..."

Silence.

Bill the Dog whined low and urgent.

The old man walked slowly to the kitchen area and looked down at the man.

The man in the chair was maybe in his mid-thirties. It was hard to tell because he had extensive scarring on one side of his face.

The old man did not recoil in horror. He had seen his share of broken and scarred bodies.

He had seen plenty of this overseas. The malignant hand of war had reached out to touch this soldier often in his lifetime.

Probably an IED.

Blew him up.

Left him scarred and broken in this house. Alone with his agonies and regrets.

The old man reached out to feel for a pulse.

There was none.

There *were* the signs of the virus. His face and lips were blueish from lack of oxygen. The dried blood and mucus on the shirt.

How had the disease found him way out here? Maybe some do-gooder social worker or someone from the VA came to check on him and carried the disease with them?

But it had found him, like it had found seemingly everyone. And now the man in the chair was gone.

Bill whined questioningly, back feet dancing on the linoleum with nervous energy.

"Sorry, buddy," the old man said softly. "He's gone."

The man in the chair had not been gone long. Maybe five or six hours. Maybe while Bill was chasing off those other dogs, this man had drawn his last fruitless breath.

The old man reached out to stroke the shaggy head of the dog.

He took his pack off and slouched down against the cabinet, pulling the dog's head into an embrace.

Dim afternoon light filtered through the pine trees and laid a yellowish-white square on the linoleum.

"I'm sorry, Bill," the old man said, burying his face into the big dog's neck and hugging Bill. "It sucks to lose family. I know."

The old man held Bill like this for several long seconds, feeling the dog's loss in the embrace.

"It'll be OK. You're still here. It'll be OK."

The old man pulled back and peered into those sad brown eyes.

"You've got me now. It'll be OK."

The dog pushed against the man and a shiver ran through the dog's large frame.

The old man repeated, "You've got me," and held him tightly.

Chapter Twelve - Service

Bill the Dog watched as the man he had brought to the house bent over and touched his fingers to the throat of the Corporal. He let the man touch the Corporal. He knew the man was trying to help. But Bill also knew that the Corporal was gone. He could smell that the body was without life. He knew death when he smelled it. He had smelled death many times when he and the Corporal were deployed in the war.

That the Corporal was gone worried Bill. The Corporal was his man, his reason, his mission, and his duty – his pack leader.

He was not sure what to do. Without the Corporal, he was unsure of his purpose. He was unsure of this new man, here, in the Corporal's house, touching the Corporal's body. He had brought this man here to help the Corporal. But it was too late. The life breath was gone now.

The old man smelled of sadness now. He dropped his pack, slouched to the linoleum floor, reached over, and hugged Bill to him. A long full embrace.

Bill could feel the man's sorrow and anger and loss. He could smell the man's worry through the myriad of smells in the kitchen.

Bill leaned into the man. Accepted his embrace. Humans needed closeness at times and right now Bill was not averse to physical closeness and comfort in worrying times.

After a long minute of being close, Bill sensed the man's tension drain. The man relaxed, released his hug, and got to his feet with a grunt.

Bill watched and listened and smelled like he had been trained to do. Bill was trained to use his senses to read a situation, to read people, and to sense threats and opportunities. It was his job.

The man checked the Corporal again. The man sighed and looked around.

Bill watched.

The man went to the living room and pulled the American Flag from the wall. Bill shifted a bit uncomfortably. How much latitude should he give this man with the Corporal's home and the Corporal's things? He followed the man as he walked around the house, checking the rooms; not too close, but close enough to observe and close enough to act, if necessary. As he was trained to do.

The man found the Corporal's uniform and medals in a bedroom and brought them out to the main room. The man draped the flag like a blanket, carefully and respectfully over the Corporal.

Not the Corporal. Bill thought. *The Corporal was dead.*

Bill knew death. He had seen men die before.

This new man talked a lot. Bill could not tell if the man was talking to Bill, or to himself. He knew some of the words and listened. Bill watched and stayed ready for those words and motions that he knew were commands. Bill watched as the old man went to the Corporal's photo on the table near the couch.

"Good looking kid," the old man said, maybe to Bill, and placed the picture on top of the flag.

On top of the Corporal's body.

As he placed the photo, the man bowed his head and said, "Sorry kid...and thank you for your service."

Bill's ear pricked. He knew the word '*Service*'. Bill's life was *service*. He had been selected as a puppy for his ability to serve. He had served well. He had spent long months being trained with the Corporal. Living with him. Eating with him. Working with him. Drilling with him.

They had deployed together. Bill and the Corporal had done their duty in the war. If not for Bill, the Corporal would not have made it out alive. Many others would have died too, if not for Bill and his training. If not for Bill's...*service*.

The old man was now looking through the Corporal's old roll-top desk in the corner.

Bill was not sure if this was right, but he watched until he could tell, or was told, otherwise.

The man shuffled through some papers and looked at photos of Bill and the Corporal.

"Lance Corporal Rick O'Neil and his military dog Sergeant Bill, Outpost Lima-6, Camp Leatherneck..." The man read out loud.

The man turned to look at Bill who was more intent now. Bill knew the man was talking to him and waited to understand what was being said.

"Sergeant? I think that means you're an officer, Bill? A Noncom?"

Bill did not answer but understood his name.

"I think military dogs always outrank their handlers, right? Something about ensuring that they are treated well?"

The man put down the photo and picked up a manual. "Department of the Navy, military dog training manual."

He looked at Bill again with a question in his eyes, "Huh... so, does this make you a sailor?"

He paged through the manual some more. "Ahhh...no...a Marine!"

Bill knew that word. And shifted up even straighter in his stance.

"Well, Marine Sergeant Bill...Thank *YOU* for *YOUR* service!" The man said with a grin and a wink. The man rolled up the manual and saluted Bill with it, then stuck it in his back pocket. "I never served...in the military anyhow...but I appreciate you guys."

The man turned back to the papers and spoke some more.

"I guess when your tour was done, you came home. Home with him. To take care of him. After the war..."

The man approached Bill and began scratching Bill's head.

"What are we going to do with you? I don't need a dog, but I can't leave a marine alone in a house with a dead man. For all I know you're a damn war hero."

The man looked out the window. He seemed to be thinking.

"It's too late now. But in the morning, you and I will give Corporal O'Neil here a decent burial and then we'll figure out what to do next."

Bill watched the man lay on the Corporal's couch and cover up with the Corporal's blanket. The smells of the two men were beginning to mix.

Bill was not sure he liked that.

He settled in to watch.

The man dropped into a snoring slumber.

Bill considered this new man. Was this his new partner? Was this his duty now?

Bill had not decided. He watched this new man sleep.

Bill stood watch as he had always done.

***

Early the next day as the sun was just breaking through the edge of the morning's darkness, the old man stirred from his slumber on the couch.

Bill lay prone, still watching, alert.

The old man rolled into an upright sitting position, rubbed his eyes, and looked around. The blanket slipped to the floor. The man jumped a bit when he saw Bill watching him.

The old man spoke in a fuzzy morning croak. "Jeez Bill, do you ever go off duty? It's a bit creepy, ya know..."

Bill watched. Bill listened. Bill did not answer. Bill was bred and trained to work. He was a working dog. Standing guard was a part of his job.

"That was a good sleep, though, haven't slept that well in a couple weeks. Maybe having a guardian angel watching over me is a good thing," the old man continued, "and not sleeping outside on the ground is always a plus!"

The old man switched to a sing-song voice that humans often use with dogs and babies. "*Huh buddy? Are you my guardian angel guard dog? Yes, you are!"*

Bill did not know if this required an answer, but he gave the man a tail wag and dipped his big head in acknowledgment.

"OK boss, I bet you have to pee," the old man continued talking. "*I have to pee*. What say we get a good pee in, eat something, and get this day started?"

Bill thumped his tail on the floor.

The old man let out a small grunt as he pushed himself up from the couch. Too many days on the move. Too many close calls. It was grinding him down. He walked to the door. Bill followed. They went outside and peed on the front lawn together.

The morning was cool. Bill heard wild turkeys waking up in their roosts and warbling in the dawn. The forest and its occupants were waking up as well. Bill sniffed the air, as if taking the forest's temperature.

Then Bill followed the old man back inside.

The old man found Bill's big bowl and filled it with Bill's food. The old man tossed a loose kibble to Bill and Bill snapped it out of the air. The old man laughed.

"You're a special one, aren't you?"

The old man found himself some food in the Corporal's cupboards and ate as well. As the old man ate dry cereal from a bowl at the kitchen counter, he read the dog training manual and mouthed words as if tasting the shape of them.

When the old man was done, he sighed and stretched a bit.

He addressed the dog. There was an unpleasant but necessary task to be done. "OK, Bill, let's give the Corporal a decent burial."

The old man went to the shed and found a shovel.

Bill watched as the old man spit on his hands and slowly began working the spade into the red dirt of the side lawn. As the morning passed, the hole got deeper and the pile of soil higher.

The old man took his time. He took breaks to drink water and eat. He wiped his face with a dish towel from the Corporal's kitchen. Digging was hard work.

But one thing was consistent. The old man continued to talk. The old man's talking came in a river of words that seemed to be more intended to make noise than to convey orders. It was like he was releasing a dammed-up flood of words that he had been holding, waiting for someone to receive them. And that someone was Bill.

The old man rested on his shovel and looked at Bill the way someone might look at a friend, across a table, over a beer in a pub, telling a story. "I'm not as young as I used to be and I'm really not cut out for this kind of work, but it has to be done and I'm the one who has to do it, unless using a shovel is another one of your tricks?"

When he wasn't talking to Bill, the old man would talk to himself too and seemed troubled at times. Bill sensed this. Sensed the old man's troubled mind. Something was broken with this man.

Other times the old man would sing or hum, like he was puttering around the house working on a common to-do list.

Bill watched and listened and sensed and studied the man.

Eventually, the old man stopped digging and considered the hole.

"That's as good as we're gonna get, Bill. It's not perfect, but it's what we got."

The man rubbed his lower back and limped slightly as he climbed up the ramp and back into the house. He wasn't cut out for manual labor or a life of constant stress and toil, but some jobs had to be done.

Bill followed.

The old man set the photo of the Corporal on the counter and carefully folded the flag and placed it there as well. The man made a neat pile out of the folded flag, the uniform with its medals and white hat, and the framed photo of the young marine.

Bill watched as the old man grabbed the handles of the wheelchair like he had done this a thousand times.

Bill let out a low growl and tensed.

Should he let this man do this?

The old man stopped and looked at him, surprised and puzzled.

Bill was not sure if this was right or not. He knew he was supposed to protect the Corporal. But something about the corporal was no longer there. He was not sure what he was supposed to do now. He sensed the man was not a threat. But he was not sure if this was right.

The man took his hands off the chair slowly and spoke directly to Bill using the authoritative voice that humans use when they want you to do something.

"Listen, marine, I'm not going to hurt anything here. I'm doing the right thing. *We're* doing the right thing. Stand down, marine!"

Bill recognized the voice of authority and sat, erect and tight, contrite, but still wary.

"Now. Come with me. I need your help. You're his best friend, I'm guessing, so you have to help me pay respects."

The man resumed maneuvering the wheelchair out of the house and down the ramp to the open grave.

Bill followed, head low, and watched uneasily.

Gently, slowly, the man lifted the body of the Corporal into the grave. Gently, slowly, respectfully he tucked the flag, uniform, medals, and the photo into the grave.

Purposefully, he stood and called to Bill.

"Marine. Come here."

Bill came and sat uneasily.

"It's time to say goodbye, my friend," the old man said with a tired look.

Bill took a step into the hole and nosed around the flag-covered body of the Corporal. He smelled the fresh dirt smells mixing with the dead smells and he was unsettled.

The old man closed his eyes and moved his right hand, up and down, then back and forth across his chest.

They stayed like that for some long minutes. Man praying. Dog silent and watching.

Eventually, the old man opened his eyes, mouthed the word "Amen" and got to work again with the shovel.

Bill climbed out and began to pace, nervously, at the edge. Bill did not feel right. He felt like he had lost something. He felt like there was something he needed to do but did not know what it was. Bill was anxious. He whined low and forlorn. He let small, plaintive barks squeeze out, despite his training to hold fast in the face of death and loss.

"I know Buddy, I know..." The old man said consolingly as he packed the dirt down with the flat of the shovel. "Let's go wash up. We'll head out in the morning."

The man lowered himself creakily to one knee and took Bill's big head into his hands. He looked deeply into Bill's forlorn eyes.

Bill felt a *connection* then.

"We'll figure this out, brother. You have to trust me. We'll figure this out together."

With that, Bill followed his...*new* man into the house.

Chapter Thirteen - Partners

The old man spent the rest of the day with Bill. They were feeling each other out. Learning each other.

The old man was sore and tired from the day's digging. He figured another day of rest could help him recover. Another night of good sleep inside wouldn't hurt either.

A couple more good meals to refuel.

Bill seemed less concerned now but was still following the old man around. Right on his heels most of the time. Watching him.

"You're wrapped pretty tightly there, marine," the old man observed, after turning around and almost tripping over Bill. "If we're going to hang out together, you're going to have to give me some space."

The old man could swear the dog understood him sometimes. He felt sorry for the dog. There was a sense of sadness about the poor thing now.

He really couldn't be mad at it.

But what was he going to do with it?

He remembered the military dog training manual and spent the early afternoon in the yard experimenting with different commands.

The dog was amazingly well-trained.

It could heel on a leash or off like a pro. It would sit, down, stay, hold, and all the other commands that the old man could give.

The only wrinkle was that the commands in the manual were in German. The old man did not speak any German and had to guess at the pronunciation. He experimented, watching how the dog responded. As a military dog, there were also commands to search and to attack.

Not for the first time, the old man wished for the internet so he could Google some of the more complex commands. Find out some of the things he should know about this dog's training. It felt a bit like he had a fancy new device and limited instructions on how to use it.

But the dog was good. The dog understood things quickly and worked well.

By the end of that first training session, the manual was well-creased. They had an introductory command of the instructions – a series of German words and hand motions that covered the basic needs of communication of intent.

"Well, Bill... if I have to be trapped with a dog in the apocalypse, I guess a well-trained dog is a good option."

The dog seemed to be enjoying this. Like it gave him something to do. Like it was in his comfort zone.

Almost like he was showing off a little.

The dog showed occasional signs of something akin to melancholy. He would look to where the Corporal was buried, as if he were trying to remember something, before laying down with a loud dog sigh.

The leaves in the trees rustled, pulling both man's and dog's attention. A cold front was fast approaching.

The wind rose up like a cold broom sweeping the last of the summer's warmth out of the woods. It looked like it might snow.

The old man suppressed a shiver and led Bill back inside.

He thought about lighting a fire in the wood stove. It looked functional. But he knew on a cold windy day like this, you'd be able to smell the smoke for miles. He didn't need to attract company.

The gas in the kitchen stove was still working. The old man improvised a stir-fried meal with some rice, a can of soup, canned tuna, cooking oil, and old carrots from the pantry.

He offered some to the dog. Bill the Dog wasn't interested and gave the old man a derisive look after sniffing.

"Hey, you can't be choosy in the apocalypse!" The old man informed Bill. "Everybody eats like a poor college student now!"

Bill did not look convinced and consoled himself by eating his own food from his own bowl.

"Now what am I going to do about food for you, dog? We might be going three to four days between towns, so we'll have to carry it somehow..." The old man looked at the big bag of dog food on the counter and frowned.

He returned his attention to the cast iron skillet and stirred his steaming concoction.

"Bill, I don't think I can carry enough food to keep you alive without killing myself. Bit of a Sophie's Choice there, Buddy. We'll have to figure something out."

Bill looked at him from his spot on the floor.

"Any chance you have a cart you can pull? You know, like a donkey cart? Don't they do that with dogs? No?"

The old man finished cooking and ate his meal silently over the kitchen sink.

His mind ranged across all that lay behind and before him now. His life, as it was, was gone now. The world, as it was, was gone now. Everyone he knew, everyone he had left was probably gone now.

He still had that one hope. That his son Paul was still in this world. That hope kept him going. That hope was big enough to keep him moving west.

Strangely, he was beginning to adjust to this new life.

Moving daily like a specter through the old world, running every day down the back roads and trails of this dead world was his life. Like he was sneaking through a museum, and at every corner expecting to be shushed or caught and ambushed by ghosts.

He was adjusting to the strangeness of it. The adventure of it.

God help him, he felt pretty good today.

He thought, "That's what makes humans successful. They adapt and make the best of the situation. They keep going."

If only Paul had found the mental and physical reserves to keep going too. The old man would find him. The old man would find his son one way or another. He needed that now.

And now he had a new partner. This big, smart, probably dangerous, dog.

Bill the Dog. The old man smiled at the thought. Trapped in the apocalypse with a dog named Bill. It was absurdist comedy at its best!

He bent over and gave Bill a scratch behind his curly ears. Bill gave the old man an adoring and adorable look.

"You're a dandy, Bill. How did you get so pretty in this crazy world?"

Bill thumped his big, feathery tail one or two times on the floor in response.

Shaking himself out of his reverie, the old man wondered out loud, "I wonder why the gas still works? Probably bottled gas this far out. Stand-alone system. I guess sometimes the world leans in your favor, even in the apocalypse and I'm not going to complain about it."

The old man found a large pot and put some water on to boil. He could fill up that big kitchen sink with hot water, find some soap and shampoo, and get cleaned up a little.

The wind outside pushed pine branches against the house. The sun began to fade lower into the trees.

The old man decided it would be best to do a bit more exploring in the house before he lost the light. He had been through it once, but now that the Corporal had been laid to rest, and they had eaten, he could take a deeper look with fresh eyes. He might find something to help him on the road ahead, especially now that he apparently had a partner in crime.

In a back closet, he found some of the Corporal's old fatigues that he could probably make fit. A little loose, but the old man didn't have much meat on him, so everything was loose these days. The camouflage coloring would be a plus, though, he thought.

In a box he hadn't opened on his first pass, the old man found the dog's military equipment, including a large harness with packs built into it. He turned to Bill, who was, as usual, sitting a few feet away, watching, and held the harness up to size the dog.

"C'mere, dog."

Bill stood and trotted over.

The old man slipped the pack harness over the dog's back and snapped it into place.

"Well, well, well, Sgt. Bill. Looks like you'll be carrying your own stuff!"

Bill sat back down, like none of this was particularly new or interesting. The old man moved on to inspect the Corporal's guns. There were three long guns and a pistol in a gun case, which was open.

Two shotguns and a rifle, with boxes of ammo stored below. He lifted one of the shotguns out of the case and held it, hesitantly.

The old man was not a gun enthusiast. In fact, this open display of armament would have caused panic in the city where he grew up. But, down here in these Georgia woods, he knew it was the norm.

He wasn't afraid or offended. He knew how to use a gun. He had fired guns. He just wasn't brought up with them. They weren't part of his life.

He returned the shotgun to the case. "Too heavy," he said to no one. "Would slow me down." He considered a pistol but thought it too was heavy as well, especially with the ammo.

He weighed the pros and cons. There were dangerous people in the world now. They were aggressive and unconstrained by the old laws and norms. They would be armed. Could he afford not to be?

But he needed to stick to his strengths. The things that differentiated him. He wasn't great with guns and having one might be more of a risk to him than a savior.

What made him different was that he could move fast and stay ahead of, and out of the way of trouble. Carrying a heavy pistol and enough ammo to make it worthwhile would slow him down. It would also lessen the food, water, and supplies he could carry.

Best to stick to his strengths. He reluctantly put the pistol back in the case, closed the door, locked it, and put the key in his pocket.

They returned to the kitchen. The big dog looked comfortable, almost at home, in his harness. The old man carried some long pants, a sleeping bag, and other useful supplies.

The old man filled the sink with warm water and proceeded to wash as best he could. The warm water felt good as he poured a cupful over his soapy tangle of hair and scrubbed out the knots.

He made an attempt to cut his hair and shave. He knew it was the apocalypse, and he'd just end up looking like an Appalachian Trail thru-hiker in a couple of days, but any hygiene he could scrounge up might help him survive another day, another week.

"Nothin' like a good sink bath," he said to Bill, smiling, as he was toweling dry. "Now I'm almost as pretty as you!" He tossed the towel onto Bill's head and Bill shook it off, playfully.

The old man considered the muddy dog. "I guess we need to do something about you too, huh?" The dog looked back questioningly. "You look like Pigpen from the old Charlie Brown cartoons."

The old man fished around in the cabinet under the sink and found a bottle of dog shampoo. He filled a plastic bucket with soapy water and led the dog to the bathtub in the master bathroom.

Bill reluctantly allowed the old man to give him a bath.

The dog looked miserable as the old man used a saucepan to ladle water from the bucket and soap the dog up. The bathtub was quickly stained brown as the mud and dirt rinsed from the dog's long, curly hair.

Now that they were both as cleaned up as well as possible, they were ready to hit the road.

The old man refilled his backpack with the things he needed so they could move out quickly in the morning. He filled several plastic bags with the dog's food and tucked them into Bill's pack. He unclasped the harness, slipped it off the dog, and set it near the door.

"Not a bad day, dog," the old man said, with no small amount of satisfaction, snuggling himself into a nest of blankets on the couch. "Good work done. A couple good meals. Got cleaned up." He continued to enumerate their good deeds to the watching dog. "Even got you sorted out to travel. One more good sleep and we'll head out in the morning."

He winked at the watching dog. "Don't stay up too late."

And with that, the old man rolled over and drifted off to sleep.

***

The old man sat upright, startled. It took him a moment to remember where he was. There was a dog barking. Low, angry barks interspersed with growls.

He shook his head to clear the sleep. "Jeez, Bill, what's going on? What is it?"

Bill was barking at the window that faced the side lawn. Circling and agitated, feet dancing on the wood floor, toenails clicking.

The old man quickly came to his senses and pushed to his feet. He knew better than to ignore a warning in the apocalypse. Especially this dog's warning. If Bill was worried, the old man was worried too.

"Quiet, Bill," the old man commanded in a low voice, and approached the window from the side, staying out of view. Bill sat and held nervously with low growls.

The old man peeled back one corner of the curtain to peer cautiously into the yard.

It took him a few moments to understand what he was seeing. At first, he thought it might be those feral dogs again. But on further inspection, it looked more like a group of...some sort of...brown animals.

"What the hell?" The old man muttered. "Pigs." He said with recognition. "Wild pigs."

The old man turned to look at Bill and shook his head.

"Geez-Louise Bill! You damn near gave me a heart attack."

He turned back to the window. There were probably ten of them. All different sizes. Some looked to be a couple of hundred pounds. Some had tusks, like the wild boars he'd seen in medieval tapestries. Some were smaller, juveniles.

Then he saw what the pigs were doing.

They were digging into the Corporal's grave.

"Son-uvah-bitch!" The old man swore, "Damn apocalypse! Damn Dogs! Damn People!" And finally like a new curse word, "Now, GODDAMN PIGS!"

The old man grabbed a couple of pieces of firewood from the stack next to the wood stove and hurried towards the door.

"You Stay! I'll scare 'em off."

The big dog charged for the door.

"Wait!" The old man held one hand out in a "Stop" signal, trying to remember the useful command for this moment.

"No!" and "HOLD!" were all he could come up with. He made a mental note to study that training guide more, but the dog seemed to get the gist of it. Bill reluctantly sat and obeyed.

The old man advanced off the porch towards the pigs, waving his hands and screaming obscenities.

"GET OFF, Goddam pigs! Go on! GIT!"

But the pigs did not seem scared. They seemed more angry than scared, like the old man was intruding on their business. They did not run. They bunched together and turned to face him—the big, tusky ones moved to the front.

The old man launched a piece of firewood at them. It bounced off the back of one of the big ones. The pig squealed in indignation and surged forward.

"Go on! Get off, you ugly mothers! Git outta here!"

The big boars started to rush at him, and he quickly backpedaled towards the safety of the porch, launching the second piece of wood in their direction.

But they were angry now. They weren't running away. They were charging towards him.

He scrambled back onto the porch and up to the front door as the angry pigs menaced him.

The old man pulled the door open that Bill the Dog was pushing and barking at. Before the old man could remember the commands to 'stay' or 'hold', the big dog had pushed by and launched himself at the pigs.

In an instant, the dog was on the attack, growling, barking, and biting at them. It was a chaotic melee. The pigs were surprised. They ran in chaotic circles, grunting and screaming in a terrible cacophony.

Bill seemed to know he was outnumbered and backed away, circling the pigs. He darted in to nip at them and danced back. In the process, the dog gradually distracted and led the invaders further away from the house and the old man.

Bill kept them busy, staying out of reach and leading them away from the grave as well. The pigs organizing against the new threat circled together for defense and the large tuskers launched at the harassing dog.

The old man regained himself and sprinted inside the house to the back room and the gun case. He dug into his pockets for the key and with shaking hands jammed it into the case lock. He flung it open and grabbed the rifle and a box of shells, cradling the gun and trying to chamber bullets as he ran back towards the porch.

He could hear the fight. The unworldly squealing of the pigs, the fighting growls of the big dog.

He managed to chamber a round, dropping the rest on the floor in the process. He checked the safety and jumped back through the door.

Bill was keeping them busy. He wasn't tangling with them directly. The big boars were dangerous and even a big dog like Bill couldn't face a pack of them in direct combat. Instead, he stayed out of reach, scoring points when he could find an opening.

The pigs circled up like a herd of bison with their toothy snouts facing out towards the skirmishing dog. They wouldn't give ground, and Bill wouldn't leave them alone.

The old man wasn't a gun guy. He knew he couldn't risk just firing into the scrum. So, he plunged forward holding the rifle like a spear, pressed the barrel against the nearest pig, and pulled the trigger. There was an explosion, and the rifle kicked back into his side, painfully.

The shot pig screamed and writhed on the ground, thrashing with pain and panic.

The others ran. Bill followed closely, pressing his attack, unfazed by the gunshot.

The old man collapsed into a sitting position, holding his bruised side, scrambling like a wounded crab back towards the porch. He frantically searched the ground for another cartridge he could get into the firing chamber.

But it wouldn't be necessary. The pigs were long gone, and Bill came bounding back from the trees, looking satisfied.

"You're a laugh a minute, dog," the old man said. "What's next? Lions? Tigers? Bears?" Then he added *"Oh my!"* as an afterthought, because it amused him to do so.

The big dog sniffed the body of the pig that had been shot. It had stopped breathing. The old man shook his head. "Bacon for dinner, I guess, huh Bill?"

The pigs had not done much damage to the grave. The old man had to do some thinking about how to keep them from digging up the Corporal again. At first, he thought about covering the grave with boards or tree logs, but he figured the pigs would just dig through them.

He considered piling up big stones like a Scythian Kurgan, but there wasn't enough stone around and he didn't know if he could handle the process himself without herniating a disk.

He supposed he could just leave and not worry about it, but something about this dog made him want to do better...*to be better*.

What could he do to secure the grave and keep those scavengers out?

The old man considered the handicap-capable van under the awning. He went back to the house to find the keys.

The old man dug two parallel trenches, just deep enough to roll the van's wheels into and not have much space between it and the ground. He drove the van over the grave and then let the air out of the tires. Two tons of metal and plastic settled into the soft, red, Georgia dirt.

"That should do it, Bill," he said to the dog, who was watching, interested.

The old man took Bill back inside and cleaned him up again with water from the sink.

The dog seemed to have avoided injury. It was good for Bill that he was smart enough to keep his distance. Those pigs would gore you, gash you, even kill you with their tusks and teeth if given half a chance.

The dog apparently was not all brawn, he had some brains too.

He cleaned the dog bite on his leg, applied some disinfectant spray, and bandaged it. It was healing nicely and wouldn't stop him from traveling.

***

The old man settled the pack harness onto the shoulders of the big dog and cinched it into place. He stretched, bending over to stretch his back and legs, hands reaching to touch his toes, or as near to his toes as he could get. He straightened up and settled his own pack into place. He looked at the dog. Then up into the grey sky.

"Come on, partner," he said to the dog, then turned and began walking.

After a minute of walking to warm up his legs, he eased into his run, heading down the dirt road west.

He could feel the stretch of the skin against the new bandage on his calf as he ran. He had been steadily accumulating scrapes and bruises over the last few weeks and needed to make sure he stayed on top of his wound care. As a doctor, he knew an infection could be as deadly as a bullet now.

Come to think of it, he'd need to check the dog over to make sure the pigs hadn't done any damage. *'Nothing dirtier than a wild animal bite.'* He thought.

The old man felt the slow, steady smack of his feet on the earth. He felt his heart beating out a familiar cadence in his chest, pulsing blood through his body. He breathed deep in through his nose, filling his chest and abdomen. He exhaled long and slow.

He felt the energy of the earth as he always did when he ran.

He felt the comfort of the dog trotting beside him and smiled a little. The dog was growing on him. He felt an affinity for it, a comradeship. Just a couple of days together and they had already lived their share of adventures.

This new world was growing on the old man. He felt some distance growing between himself and the great pile of bones.

Maybe he would find some purpose in this world yet.

Maybe he would find something to live for.

Maybe he...and this dog... would find Paul.

Chapter Fourteen - Run

December 14th – Six weeks since the virus ended the world…

Janet ran.

The obscenities pouring from the man she had just left bleeding in the dirt faded away…

Like the man himself.

He was nothing. He was a threat that had been dealt with.

Like she always dealt with threats.

She had the hard skills, built up over years of practice. She could dominate most situations. Her force of will bent others to her path.

If they didn't bend, they got run over or shoved aside.

She was KJ the Killer.

Until now her fights had been in the courtrooms, in the conference rooms, and in the partners' offices. Not in the dirt. She had emasculated plenty of men, but never had to elbow them in the windpipe or kick them in the groin as part of the process.

Could the physical act of defending herself simply be a logical extension of who she had always been? The world wasn't playing by the rules anymore. Why should she?

She ran.

It felt good. In this dead world, the visceral effort made her feel alive. She felt the animal joy of exertion.

She was breathing hard. Her lungs were still scarred with the vestiges of the virus. Her legs protested. The motion felt mechanical. She felt heavier than she should have. But she stuck with it and settled into a stride, oblivious to the discomfort.

She had always been an athlete. It was part and parcel of the way she defined herself. She had been the captain of the volleyball team in college. Janet ran the offense and was the 'setter.' They hadn't won the championship, but they had overachieved.

At just about six feet tall, Janet was a physical presence on the court. She was not gangly and uncoordinated like some tall young women whose late-teenage growth spurts overwhelm their physical control. She was strong and athletically built; and this, combined with her mental focus, made her a force—a force of will that nearly carried her team to the championship.

She covered the court with a relentless tenacity, feeding her 'hitters' with brutal efficiency. To watch her spike a quick hit into the opposition was like watching an eagle dive and take a fish.

The fish never stood a chance once the eagle locked in.

Now, as she thought back to those days on the court, in the zone, she poured that energy into her protesting legs.

Her mind returned to the physical act as her body reminded her of the effort.

More of the adrenaline from the fight drained from her system.

She could have stopped at that point. The man who attacked her was far behind and could not catch up. That man was not a threat. He had never really been a threat once she had decided to deal with him.

Her life bubbled up unbidden from her subconscious like a series of still pictures.

A painful image of a smiling wedding photo flashed by.

'Oh, Ted!' The love of her life. Her partner in marriage and so much more. He was the anchor, the steadiness that enabled her to do what she did every day in her career.

She remembered the wedding. It had been at a boat house by the river on a beautiful day. They were so young, but they were happy. They were no more than kids just out of school, preparing to launch into the adventure of a shared life.

Ted never stood a chance once Janet decided he was *the one*. Once she had him in her sights the marriage was a forgone conclusion.

Another painful image flashed by.

It was of her slipping away from Ted and the kids and their warm Sunday morning bed cuddle to head out for a work conference. The little one said, "Stay, Mommy. You're always working. Stay with us, Mommy."

Those pleading eyes could melt the coldest heart. She had leaned in for a hug and a kiss and a promise of pancakes when she got back.

Did she sacrifice for them?

No. She got things done.

Did they sacrifice for her?

Probably. But they were always *team Janet*. And thanks to her family, she had lived with purpose.

They were gone. What was her purpose now?

She shook her head to clear the images. Regret of time not spent had no use in this world.

Her new focus would be survival. To put emotion and soft things aside. There might be time for memorials later but now was the time to push all that down and use her hardened skill set to stay alive.

Death and chaos weren't just in the city she knew now. They were *everywhere*.

There was no going back.

Her heart was pumping hot blood to her face. Her breathing was ragged but rhythmic as the wind whipped her black hair into her eyes.

She reached back and tied a quick ponytail, a well-practiced move that she could do without breaking stride.

A tree had fallen across the trail ahead. The trunk of the tree was horizontal and a couple feet off the ground.

Without hesitation, she reached out, planted her hands on the rough bark, and vaulted over.

She felt the strength in her shoulders and back. The satisfying launch and thump as she flew and landed like a gymnast would.

Janet wiped the grit from her hands and kept running. Slower now as the tiredness accumulated. The anger and hate had drained from her body and a new set of convictions was rising.

A confidence that she had advantages now. She had a physical and mental toolkit that was honed to deal with hard things. She thought back to the confidence she had always had and how she had used it to succeed.

The class action lawsuits she had won for the plaintiffs, and for the firm. Those other lawyers - braying prep-school boys who thought their Fortune 500 clients offered them some sort of protection. They thought they had the resources to beat her in open battle.

She used that overconfidence against them. When they brought their big resources and budgets to bear on her, she would have already side-stepped their attack and slipped in for the kill.

The cases she had enjoyed taking down the most were the doctors, as they sat smug and unassailable in depositions; not nervous, not scared. Those doctors acted mostly disinterested, like they were above this petty proceeding, calm in their sense of self-superiority.

They saw her, not with fear or hate or derision. They saw her as an ant on the sidewalk. A pest. They were so certain that they were working for the greater good.

That *they were* the greater good.

That the pain, suffering, and accidental death caused by their devices and drugs were for the greater good. That those people's lives were a necessary rounding error in a great march of progress led by gods.

She lived for that moment when she saw the realization come over them. That they were going to be held accountable. You could see and feel the change as their god-like confidence cracked.

The firm took their money. She took their confidence. She took their careers. And more often than not, she took their manhood.

KJ the Killer evened the score, one dethroned medical god at a time.

She exhaled deeply and started to walk. She was breathing hard and her back hurt from the effort.

Was there sense to any of this? She wondered why the virus hadn't taken her like it had taken everyone she knew and loved?

Maybe because she was too mentally and physically strong for it.

Maybe because it recognized a fellow killer.

Or maybe it was just morbid dumb luck.

She also knew that you make your own luck. You prepare, you train, you react and make your move without hesitation.

The "unlucky" hesitate and second guess.

They don't survive.

The virus gave one last tug at her and dragged up a rough cough and a mouthful of phlegm that she gagged on and spat onto the trail.

She cleared her throat. Traces of that thing were still in her lungs. But her body had found it, identified it, and killed it. She was getting back to full health. Just a bit of residual cough and fatigue.

She wiped the sweat from her brow and walked.

She was still here.

The virus couldn't kill her. The chaotic mess of this new world couldn't kill her.

She was still here.

KJ the Killer.

Chapter Fifteen - Not-So-Innocent

December 17th – Six and a half weeks since the virus ended the world...

Janet smelled steam. The unmistakable rusty smell of steam from an overheated vehicle. A camper van was off the road ahead with steam pouring from its open hood.

Janet was not afraid. Nor was she curious. If they left her alone, she would leave them alone. If they were a threat, well, then she'd deal with them. If there was an opportunity, she'd take it.

KJ the Killer took a deep breath and moved in.

A sharp wind evaporated the sweat from Janet's arms. She felt a chill, like a passing ghost. Her heart settled from a hard drumbeat in her chest to a low rhythmic thump as she walked.

She wiped her eyes with the sleeve of her shirt and looked ahead at the vehicle on the road. What was going on with this overheated camper van?

It was an older, boxy model. The hood was propped open, and she could smell the metal of the overheated radiator.

Janet could hear snippets of an argument as she cautiously approached. It was hard to get all of it. The wind was gusting, creating white noise that washed out the voices, making them fade in and out like a bad phone connection.

She approached the van on the opposite side from where the people were arguing. Better to stay unnoticed. Was this even something that she wanted to get involved with?

She had a choice to make. She could either make her presence known or just keep going. The way they were arguing they would probably never notice.

Or she could make her presence known and see what was going on. Her recent experience, however, had shown that the world she knew had changed. In these dark days after the great dying, people were...strange. People were unhinged from the anchors of civilization.

People had become dangerous, devolving into the dark parts of their nature. Threatened, they looked out for themselves, and their basic humanity took a back seat.

She heard a woman and a man and pieces of the conversation.

"I told you something was wrong!" The woman said in a nagging tone.

"So, you're the expert now?" The man shot back, sarcastically.

"What the hell are we supposed to do now?" The woman again.

Janet moved into the shadow of the van.

The van blocked the conversation, and she was getting less of it now, but the tone seemed to be more heated.

"We had a deal!" The man yelled, as if to win a point.

Then, some garbled exchange Janet couldn't catch.

"Not the girl!" The woman clearly yelled.

A movement out of the corner of Janet's eye caught her attention. A curtain shifted in the van window, and she thought she saw a small hand.

For a moment, Janet thought, '*Oh my God, a child in this mess*.' But then considered the situation, '*Don't be distracted. Just deal with this problem.'*

KJ came around the corner of the van just as the man half-pushed, half-cuffed the woman to the ground. The woman, cowering, scrambled out of the dust to stand with her back against the van, her arms up for protection.

The door to the van was open and a toolbox lay spilled on the ground.

KJ could have just kept going, but this was a bully. And she hated bullies.

"Hey!" KJ interjected.

The altercation stopped as they both visibly jumped at this intrusion. The man turned and tensed.

"Is there a problem here?" KJ asked, matter-of-factly.

The man was big. Not just fat, which he was as well, but big. One of those solid fat men who carried their weight like a weapon. He had short, light brown hair with a bald spot and piggish eyes in a small red face.

In contrast, the woman was scarecrow-skinny, in jeans and a flannel shirt with her back against the van.

"Who the hell are you?" The man replied, looking around to see if anyone else was with Janet.

All he saw was a woman - alone in the apocalypse.

KJ did not respond but began to circle slowly in a balanced stance like she had been taught.

The man gave one last shove and released the woman's shirt from his sausage-fingered grip.

"You best mind your own business, darlin'," he said, turning to face Janet.

"I decide what is my business," KJ replied in a low voice, almost a growl, without emotion.

The man looked Janet up and down. He stared into her eyes and smiled a small, smug smile.

Never once breaking this fix on Janet, he pulled the scrawny woman up straight like a rag doll and slapped her hard across the face with his free hand. The woman collapsed into the dirt, crying through a split lip.

"What are you going to do, sweetie?" His smile broadened. "You gonna stop me? You gonna kick my ass? You gonna call the *Po-lice*?"

But Janet never heard these questions. Janet was gone. Only KJ stood here now - a calmness flowing through her as she settled into the confidence of her killer persona.

This was a part of her nature. It had always been a part of her nature. When there was a moment of truth, in the courtroom or in a game, Janet became a different person, or more precisely, a window opened on a part of her that was a different person. She shifted in these instances and became the most capable part of herself.

Time slowed, and everything came into focus. Some people called it 'the zone.'

KJ felt it now. KJ the Killer may have smiled a little bit. She didn't like this man, and she was quite certain she could run circles around him. He was an overconfident pig of a man, and she wouldn't take shit from him.

The scrawny woman sobbing on the ground entreated, "Leave her alone, Karl."

"Yeah, Kaaarrl..." Janet drawled out his name mockingly. "Step back before you get hurt."

Karl snapped at the fallen woman, "Shaddup! Stay out of it!" and turned to confront Janet.

KJ circled in to only a few feet away. She was ready for him and expected he would make a charge at her – and then she could drop him like the piece of filth he was.

"Why don't you calm down and walk away, Karl?" KJ said, in a calm, weighted voice, the one she used to make her opponents doubt themselves.

But apparently, Karl had an animal nature too. He stared at Janet - an animal fury behind his eyes. He seemed to come to some decision and lunged for Janet, trying to grab her.

She was prepared for the aggression.

KJ was moving even as he took his first step. Like a bullfighter, she pivoted out of his oncoming grasp.

Using his momentum against him, she sidestepped his charge and shoved him in the back as he rushed past. The move left him grasping at thin air where she had been moments before.

Then, with practiced flow and efficiency, she kicked the side of his knee for the coup de grâce.

But something was wrong.

In her mental movie of that move, it went differently. When she had practiced it with her instructor, in the city, his leg was supposed to buckle, dropping him hard to the mat.

Not this man. He just grunted. He didn't buckle. He didn't budge! It was like kicking a tree trunk.

Karl turned quickly for a big man, even angrier now. Wild fury raged in his eyes. KJ had overestimated her ability and her advantage over the fat man.

He managed to grab at her shirt and pulled her hard, dragging her as he stumbled. His other hand lashed out and grabbed a fistful of her hair, yanking viciously.

Shards of pain flashed sharply behind Janet's eyes. KJ brought her knee up hard, targeting the groin as she had been taught, but Karl seemed to be expecting this and grabbed her knee as it came up, twisting her, lifting her off her feet, and slamming her down onto her back.

The wind was knocked out of her. More than that, she was shocked that she had been knocked down by this man. Panic began to climb up the back of her brain like a poison monkey.

KJ's mind raced, and she frantically searched for a way out of this mess. Panic gripped her. She tried to roll away. She looked around for anything she could use as a weapon, but the man dropped his weight to pin her to the ground, straddling her. His vicious pig eyes burned with fury over her.

"Not so tough now, girly!" He snarled.

She struggled, punching and clawing, trying to find a soft spot. The man grabbed her hands. He was too big to move and too strong for her to break free.

Then the other woman jumped on his back, attacking from behind, pounding and scratching and screaming like a demented wraith. But even with all her berserker fury, she was a wisp of a woman and was no more than an annoyance to this bull of a man.

Karl lashed out from his kneeling position at the woman on his back, swinging his arm and knocking her back.

But he was distracted, and his weight shifted. KJ pushed hard with her feet and managed to wriggle free, scrambling away in the dirt like a crab.

Just as Karl, was turning back to Janet...

BANG!

An explosion cracked through the air. Everything stopped.

There was the brief brimstone smell of gunpowder in the air before it was carried away and dissipated by the swirling wind.

A stunned KJ watched as Karl clutched at the side of his face, shocked. He pulled his hands away and looked at the blood in amazement. Part of his ear was missing. Blood oozed from the side of his head, and he screamed in feral anger.

A girl, maybe eight years old, lay sprawled in the van doorway with a smoking shotgun as big as herself.

The girl lay there, wide-eyed and terrified.

Next to Karl, the scrawny woman was screaming uncontrollably, sobbing and wiping Karl's blood from her flannel shirt.

KJ used the chaos to get back to her feet.

Karl was screaming at the girl now, holding his hand to the side of his head where buckshot had torn into his ear and cheek, and where blood was now streaming.

But he wasn't out of the fight. If anything, he was even angrier now. He struggled to his feet and staggered towards the van door where the girl was sprawled with the gun, looking stunned.

"You little shit!" Karl bellowed.

The girl shrank back away from him as he approached, a look of sheer terror on her face, like a scared, beaten puppy.

KJ was back in a crouch now and it was her turn to be angry.

This guy was an asshole. This guy had laid hands on her, and now he was going after this child.

As her fury surged, she sprang into action like an avenging angel. In one continuous motion, she grabbed the empty toolbox, advanced on Karl from behind, and using her momentum, swung it hard against the back of his head.

He dropped into the dirt, unconscious, like a great limp thing, moaning and bleeding.

Janet kicked him with all the force she could muster. "Stay down, a-hole," she ordered.

The woman continued to sob with distress on the ground.

KJ took the shotgun from the girl and pulled the bolt back to expose the remaining shells. She wasn't a gun enthusiast, but growing up, every farm had a shotgun, and she was familiar with the mechanics.

She systematically ejected the clip, unloaded the weapon, and kicked the remaining shells under the van. She removed the bolt, tossed the gun aside, and threw the bolt into the woods.

Karl moaned some more. KJ kicked him hard again, wincing a bit as her toe crunched against something hard.

KJ turned to confront the scrawny woman who was sobbing uncontrollably in the dust of the road. Tears blood-streaked muddy lines across her face like the tributaries of a polluted river system. Her hair was matted and wild.

KJ knelt beside the woman, grabbed her by the collar of her shirt, and pulled her face in close.

"Stop it," KJ said, looking intently into the woman's face. "We need your help."

The woman continued to sob and looked away.

"What's your name?" KJ asked.

"G...G....Grace," the woman managed to stammer between sobs.

"OK, Grace, do you have any rope or something I can tie Karl up with? Before he comes to, and we have to kick his ass again?" KJ smiled a little at this.

"I...I...don't know..." came the non-helpful answer.

At that moment, Grace stopped crying. Janet was glad she was coming around, but a different look came over her and she glared at Janet suspiciously. "What have you done to Karl?"

Janet was speechless in response to the woman's change in attitude.

Grace continued, asking, "What do you want anyhow? We was fine before you came along! Now look what you've done! Now what am I going to do?"

Janet was stunned but recovered her calm and remembered the victims she had worked with. She took a breath and looked Grace deep in the eyes. "Grace. You've been through a lot. You can do better than Karl. He's an animal. Things aren't going to get better. You need to get away from here, away from him."

Grace was unresponsive and her face took on a vacant empty look.

Janet shook her head and let go of the woman.

"OK, Grace. You're going to have to pull yourself together here. I'll see what I can find."

KJ kicked through the assorted tools in the dirt. Pipe, pliers, various wood chisels, drill bits, nails, screws, and a nice big roll of duct tape.

The universal tool.

That would do it.

In a fitting move, she hogtied the big man, taping Karl's wrists and ankles together behind his back, leaving him face down in the dirt. The blood dripping from his ear coagulated in his hair. He was lucky it was only a bird shot.

That would hold him. At least until she was out of the area. Good enough for now.

Grace had settled down and had moved back into the van to comfort the girl.

When she emerged, she had cleaned her face and put her hair back. The deep worry lines on her face and her swollen lip made her look old and worn down.

Grace considered KJ for a moment and spoke. "What now?"

"Let me ask you that question," Janet said, "What now for you?" and after a moment added, What happened here?"

Grace felt for the van stairs, sat back slowly, and looked at her hands. "Well, we were all fleeing the city after everyone started dying, and I...I met up with Karl. He offered to take me in the van. He said he was an ex-cop and that he knew a place we could go..." She trailed off weakly, looking up at Janet and lifting one hand to trace a strand of greasy bangs back with her finger.

"What about your daughter?" Janet asked.

Grace looked confused for a moment, then sad, and responded, "Oh, you mean Teri, no, she's not my daughter, we picked her up, wandering."

'Another ad hoc collection of survivors thrown together in the apocalypse', Janet thought.

KJ made her way around to the hood of the van to inspect the radiator.

She found a split in the hose and wrapped it as best she could with duct tape. She'd jerry-rigged enough machines on the farm to know this would hold for a while. How long? Who knew. But it would get the woman far enough away from here, maybe to the next town.

She rounded the van again to find Grace still seated on the stairs, but now with little Teri lying snug in her lap.

This gave her pause...but just a moment's pause.

Janet spoke, "I patched the hose as best as I could. I filled the radiator back up with creek water." She pointed through the trees. "You'll want to keep it topped off." KJ shrugged and continued. "This might get you a mile, or it might get you fifty miles, I don't know, but it will get you away from here," she said, in a tired voice. "When it starts to overheat, turn it off and let it cool, and add more water if you can. If you keep driving on it, you'll cook the engine."

A small voice came from Grace's shoulder.

"What are you going to do?" Teri asked softly, fear and uncertainty in her little voice.

"Honey, I'm going to keep moving. You and Grace are going to stick together, and you'll be fine. You'll figure it out." KJ said with a tone of finality.

Dead air hung as they waited for an explanation, but KJ offered none.

"What about Karl?" Grace asked to break the uncomfortable silence.

KJ looked at the man who lay face down in the dirt and shrugged. "He made his bed, and he can sleep in it."

Grace hesitated, unsure.

KJ nodded to the van. "Get going now and I'll take care of Karl. Find someplace to survive. Find someplace for the girl."

Grace carried Teri reluctantly into the van and started the engine. She shifted into gear and eased back onto the road.

KJ watched as the van pulled away, the face of the young girl looking out the window with haunted eyes as the dust of the road swirled and settled.

She turned to consider the prone bulk of Karl.

What was she going to do with this piece of garbage?

She could kill him. She could leave him here to die on his own. She didn't really care either way.

She kicked through the scatter of tools. She sorted out a jackknife and a box cutter. She pushed back the sleeve of the box cutter to reveal the rusty razor blade. She threw both deep into the woods.

"Don't want to make it too easy, you dumb pig." she said to the unconscious Karl. He could probably, with enough effort, escape the duct tape ligature, but if he couldn't, then the world would be a better place.

With that, KJ turned away and resumed walking west.

She noticed a slight pain in her toe as she started to jog. She looked down to see a rusty spot of blood seeping out of her athletic shoe. She must've torn a flap off when she kicked that son-of-a-bitch, and the running had aggravated it.

KJ the killer. A flesh and blood killer with feet of clay. She'd have to find some better shoes and maybe a Band-Aid.

She thought about this encounter. *'That was dreadful,'* she decided. Things were the same everywhere. She'd have to be more cautious in the future if she wanted to survive.

All the loss and death was too much to bear. It made it hard for her to think. She needed to push that down.

Build a wall.

Simplify.

All she had to do now was survive.

Chapter Sixteen – Burying the Past

Why hadn't she stayed with Grace and Teri? She could have. Janet probably should have stayed and maintained human contact. Built a tribe or a new family. Found a way.

But she didn't. She couldn't.

The wounds were too raw. It felt too soon. Too soon to let new people in. This new world of chaos and dying had systematically torn away everyone she loved. She wasn't sure she could take it anymore. She didn't know if she was strong enough to take that chance.

An emotional shell was calcifying around her psyche, and she felt like a scared and angry child hiding in a closet from a terrible and unforgiving monster.

So, she shut the world out.

The trail emerged into a wider dirt road that showed signs of recent vehicle traffic.

She smelled the body before she saw it. She had begun to recognize that smell. The smell of offal and excrement and death.

It came from a compact car that had rolled slightly off the dirt road. The driver's side door was ajar. A bare, discolored leg extended from the interior and ended with a dirty, bloated foot resting on the ground. The driver had apparently, in one last lucid moment, tried to get out of the car, but had not made it. They had fought to the end.

More death. Janet slowly walked towards the car and its grisly occupant.

It had been a woman but was barely recognizable now. The woman's corpse was emaciated and showed signs of the virus. But oddly, as Janet examined the scene, the body seemed fresher, like it had not been here the full six to eight weeks since the great dying.

The woman's head was thrown back as if she'd been gasping for air in those final moments. Her face was ruined, cadaverous. Her shirt was a mosaic of dried blood and stains.

'A recent corpse,' Janet thought. The woman, somewhere around thirty years old, but it was hard to tell, had been dead for a few days at most.

What had transpired here? The woman fought the virus, like Janet had, and refused to die. And she had made it here. Why? Where was she going? What made her cling to life?

More questions that would never be answered. Could not be answered. Stories with no endings.

Janet shuddered and covered her face with the sleeve of her shirt. She turned away, feeling sick. In the old world, this woman might have been saved. Who knew? Maybe the local EMT's would have arrived on the scene, stabilized her, and bundled her into a medivac off to the emergency room.

Not now. Maybe never again. The EMTs were probably the first taken by the virus.

Janet thought about looking through the car for supplies. There might be something useful. But she decided not to. She couldn't stomach it. She just wanted to keep going. To get away from all this death.

A small sound startled her. She turned back to the car and the open driver's door to tentatively peer inside. She looked beyond the wrecked remains of the driver. The noise was probably an animal. A raccoon or possum scrounging for food.

But the sound, a gurgling, slight intake of breath was coming from the back seat. She had not seen anything at first. The mud-covered windows had hidden the contents of the back seat from her view. Now she peered past the corpse and what she saw made her heart break.

There was a toddler strapped in a car seat.

'Dammit.' She thought, fighting back the combination of remorse and anger. *'This goddamn world.'*

As she peered at the child in the stained car seat, she thought she saw it move. Ever so slightly. Focusing, she was sure of it now and heard the soft wet inhalation of a breath.

'Sweet Jesus.' She thought.

It was a two-door sedan. She'd need to get behind the front seats. So, she began levering the driver's - *mother's?* - corpse out of the way so she could get to the back.

A toddler, probably two or three years old. A little girl in a pink, stained sweatshirt and fouled pajama bottoms. Janet's heart fell.

The child was barely breathing. Her little head lolled to one side, and she was very pale. She was unconscious. She looked emaciated and probably dehydrated. She'd been here since the mother died. Janet put her hand on the girl's forehead, and it felt clammy, her breath shallow and rattling.

"Hang on, honey," Janet said. "I'm going to get you out of there."

The child was unresponsive as Janet unbuckled her from the car seat. A limp, wet, doll. Her short-cropped brown hair was matted and dirty.

Janet carried the little girl to an open spot and laid her down. She felt a rush of incredible sadness and helplessness as she was forced to remember her own children—children she had watched die from the plague.

She couldn't save them. So much pain. So much loss.

It was hard to imagine any future beyond these days of death, dying, and loss.

She couldn't help her children, but, maybe, she could help this one. Or at least she would try.

Janet looked around the car for the kid's bag. She took the keys out of the ignition to open the trunk. There had to be extra clothes for the child. As a mother, *she* had never gone anywhere without a bag of supplies for the kids.

In the trunk, she found a messy collection of bottles, blankets, towels, and a travel bag with wet wipes, diapers, and clothes. She carried the armful of supplies back to where the child was lying in a sheltered grassy spot away from the stench of the car.

Janet did her best to spoon-feed water and some electrolyte mixture into the unconscious child. There wasn't much she could do. She wished again for competent medical help that used to be a 911 phone call away. The medical professionals were dead. The 911 operators, even the phones, were all dead.

"We have to get you cleaned up," Janet said as much to herself as to the toddler.

The sun was setting. The orange glow of dusk crept up the horizon through the forest cover. The Earth never relented in its daily cycles of death and rebirth. The planet didn't stop turning. It stayed a constant clicking metronome of light and dark, of life and death.

Janet cleaned the child as best she could and got her into some fresh clothes. The poor little thing probably hadn't eaten in days. Her little body shivered uncontrollably trying to keep the life force. She had been out there, strapped into the back seat of a car, exposed to the elements, with the only person alive to help her lying dead behind the wheel.

Janet felt the first chill in the air and took the little girl into her arms. '*It's going to get cold tonight.*' She thought, looking with concern at the unconscious sick child. She rubbed the little girl and rocked her, singing nonsensical lullabies to comfort her. KJ the killer gave way to Janet the mother. She snuggled down into her sleeping bag with the toddler in her arms.

She felt the little girl's shallow expansion and contraction of breath against her chest. She felt the small heartbeat of life pulse through the embrace. Janet kissed the top of the little girl's head and whispered soothingly, "It's going to be ok, honey. I've got you." And she drifted into a fretful sleep filled with dreams of death and violence.

Janet was woken in the night as the little girl shook with a violent seizure. She searched her mind for some way to help. But it was too late. The little girl's body had been subjected to too much. Janet could no longer feel a heartbeat.

She knew the child was dead.

There was no breathing, no heartbeat, and the heat of life drained from the small body. The little girl had given up the fight.

Janet cried. She cried long and hard. She beat her fists into the ground and cursed God for his meanness.

How many innocents had died? This little girl would have grown up to be a friend, a lover, and even a mother herself! All the potential and love and joy of a life snuffed indiscriminately.

What was the point of living in a world that snatched all that promise away?

She never even knew the child's name.

There was some comfort.

At least the poor kid didn't have to die alone.

This new world was random and indiscriminate. Janet felt an impotent anger. Angry that she couldn't help. Angry that for all her strength and abilities she couldn't save this one child.

And that anger simmered.

She hated being forced to play the victim. She never was the victim. Sure, she didn't win every case, but when she lost, she didn't cry about it. She learned from her losses and used that as fuel for the next fight.

Janet wiped her face. She would not sit here feeling sorry and crying. This world was filled with too much sorrow, and it didn't want or need her comfort. It wanted her to fight. Like a bully in the schoolyard, it kept pushing her.

Fine. If that's what this new world took, she would fight. Fight for control. Fight for survival. Fight for herself.

***

Janet had no means to dig graves, even shallow graves for the mother and child.

In the end, she laid the little girl's body with her mother in a shallow depression next to an old farm stone wall and made a mound of stones over them.

As she stacked the stones, she built a wall against the world. She retreated to her emotional citadel.

She didn't need anyone.

Bury the past with the bones of the dead. Kill the memories. Survive.

Janet stood. She wiped the dirt and grit from her hands and clothing like a worker cleaning up after a job. She turned away.

She should have said a prayer or something, but she did not.

Sentimentality was wasted in this new world. What kind of random and specious deity did this?

KJ the killer gathered her pack and belongings. She turned from the pile of stones and grimly walked down the road.

***

It was two days later when she realized she was limping. In her dazed emotional state, she hadn't given it much thought. But eventually, the discomfort tugged hard enough at what remained of her conscious mind to get her attention.

Janet sat on a rock and pulled off the dirty shoe. She gingerly rolled the blood-stained sock off her foot to take a look.

The toe was swollen and red from where a flap of skin had been torn off. The nail was torn as well. Dirt from the road had crusted it brown, mixing with the blood like an odd cement.

For a moment, she just stared at it, not knowing what to do. She found the hunting knife and probed around the area, scraping as much of the dirt crust off as she could.

She winced. It hurt like hell.

KJ the Killer had beaten that pig Karl, but he had managed to hurt her after all.

Every action has a reaction.

The area around the toe was red, swollen, and hot to the touch. She rinsed it with some bottled water and put a fresh pair of socks on.

That would have to do. It was all she had.

Janet continued walking west. Soon the discomfort from the toe was nagging at her again. It seemed to be rubbing against the side of the shoe and that was aggravating it.

Once more, she took the shoe off and thought about what to do, how to relieve the pressure. Once more, she took out the knife. This time, with some difficulty, she used the blade to cut the side of the shoe out. Now there was a rough opening in the top and side of the shoe and there was nothing to rub against.

Janet resumed walking west on the dirt road. The hole she carved in the shoe helped. Without the rubbing, she was able to make progress until the sun was setting.

A sign told her she was now in Tennessee.

That night, she made camp under the Tennessee stars. With the cities and streetlights gone dark, the stars shone in all their brightness and splendor. In a different circumstance, it would have been magnificent to her, like a mad celestial artist had thrown a bucket of brilliance against the night's canvas.

She huddled in her sleeping bag, pushing thoughts of the child who had recently shared it with her out of her hardened, sealed-off mind. Fitful sleep came to her marred by nightmares and the throbbing in her foot.

In the morning, she could barely stand. On inspection, the toe was more swollen, and red striations ran away from it into the foot. She broke a branch and fashioned a walking stick to help her keep moving.

After a few painful hours of slow, limping progress she knew she'd need to stop.

'Dammit!' She thought. *'I'm stuck in the middle of nowhere and there's no help.'* She had a pang of regret. If she had stayed with Grace and Teri, they might have been able to help her.

Janet had decided to make her way alone. Decided that she didn't need anyone. But maybe, just maybe, this cold, spinning, seemingly uninvested world had other ideas.

Toward noon, she looked for a place to stop. Someplace she wouldn't be noticed. Everyone she'd met so far had been dangerous and she was in no condition to defend herself. Maybe if she rested. Stayed off the foot. It would get better. Or at least, improve enough for her to limp somewhere she could find a first aid kit.

As she inched her way up an incline, something blue caught the corner of her eye. There were some tarps off the road. It looked like some sort of abandoned construction site.

Maybe she could find a med kit. Maybe she could hide there until her foot at least recovered enough to walk some more.

Chapter Seventeen - The Dig

January 1st – Eight weeks since the virus ended the world…

The old man kept a slow but steady pace down the gravel road. It was getting on in the day and he needed to start thinking about shelter for the night.

Bill the Dog trotted about ten yards ahead as the vanguard.

A small dust cloud rose behind them marking their progress.

The old man thought about that.

He'd been keeping away from main roads to avoid interacting with what was left of humanity. These fire roads were easier on the feet anyhow and presented opportunities for hunting and gathering. He kept a good pace going with his easy dogtrot, walking and resting when needed.

Bill the Dog had become a surprisingly good partner during the few days since they had left the Corporal's house and headed west.

The dog had not been any trouble. He had been able to keep up just fine with an easy, economical dogtrot of his own.

Food and water hadn't been any problem either. The dog carried his own food and seemed to be able to stomach everything the old man threw his way. Although he did seem somehow offended by the dried kibble, and only obliged to eat it with a begrudging attitude.

Bill was finicky but practical. The local streams were full, and Bill and the old man certainly didn't go dry.

But even more importantly, the dog was a great early warning system.

Bill had a good nose and sharp ears and could sense things ahead in their path well before the old man would notice.

Not only would the dog sense the presence of others, but he would also alert the old man by stopping and staring in the direction of the unknown presence. It was some artifact of the dog's training and was proving especially useful.

Of course, the old man knew that dogs, in general, had keener ears and eyes than humans but it still seemed like a magic trick. Bill would become aware of human activity and freeze before the old man had any inkling. Which meant the old man could "see" things before they saw him.

Which was handy.

Even so, the old man was still trying to differentiate the dog's alerts.

When they stopped to rest, the old man would practice the German commands from the training manual. The manual was starting to shred from constant use and the abuse of riding rolled up in the old man's back pocket. The pages bent and tearing out. But he was starting to learn the dog's language and that could come in handy. That could save both their lives.

It wasn't just *live* humans that the dog sensed. Bill would alert for bodies or abandoned cars or houses near the trail as well. Anything not part of the natural environment would cause Bill to stop and alert.

"I wish you could just tell me exactly what you're worried about," he had said, the second or third time the dog alerted for an abandoned house or road crossing. "But I suppose I'll learn how to read your signals ... eventually..."

This dog had probably saved his life already, so it was worth the extra caution to take him seriously when he sensed something ahead of them. The old man just wished Bill could be more specific.

There weren't many human travelers left in this dead world, but the old man wanted to avoid them if he could. His recent experiences with what was left of humanity almost cost him his life.

In their few days on the trail together, they had seen just one man. Bill had alerted moments before the old man himself heard the sound of an engine. They had concealed themselves in the woods and watched the man pass on an ATV.

The old man was worried that the dog might bark or give chase, but he did not. Bill lay silent and watchful with the old man, not making any noise.

"Good boy," the old man said as the threat passed in a cloud of dust down the dirt road.

Knowing that the dog would give a warning when strangers were around was comforting.

It was quite useful, actually.

It gave the old man an advantage.

To be prepared for something. To choose whether he wanted to interact with another survivor. Which, so far, he had not.

He had no reason to. He had everything he needed. He didn't need help.

There were no neutral interactions anymore. These strangers would either be dangerous or needy or sick. He didn't have material, time, or energy for that.

He had done his time in the real world, and it had taken everything from him.

He didn't owe this world anything.

He needed to keep moving west and find Paul.

The old man was making good time now. He and Bill the Dog covered fifteen to twenty miles a day. He could do more, especially on a good road, but he didn't want to use himself up. He had to take time to find food and make sure he was giving himself enough time to recover.

He was already painfully thin from his pre-pandemic life. The fact was things hadn't really changed much for him.

Before the virus, when he was running the long trails, he fit right in.

Ultrarunning was a sport filled with broken misfits. Ex-drug addicts, ex-alcoholics, and others who needed the comforting pain of running excess to stay clean and cling to what little bit of sanity they had left.

That was him.

Clinging to sanity.

Waking up every day and having to make up a reason to keep going.

If that reason was a hundred-mile run with his new, strange friends, then so be it. The all-consuming experience of staying on your feet far into the mountain trails, long into a second day of continuous forward movement kept him alive and tamped down the demons.

In the running world that he adopted...or that had adopted him, he was the ultra-running doctor. Or ex-doctor. The trail runners called him "Old Doc". They didn't care about his past. They didn't measure him by the rates he would charge or the papers he had written. They didn't care that he had been ruined by lawyers and barred from practicing.

In the sweaty dust of an all-day run, he was just another vessel in the storm, afraid or unable to make port.

Who could have guessed that this last-ditch effort to maintain sanity would turn into a useful survival skill?

Now he still ran the dirt roads. But he ran alone. More alone than he had ever been. Except now this damn dog was here.

Funny how the world worked. I wouldn't leave you alone. Even dead the world kept poking at you.

He had considered getting a bicycle or even a scooter of some sort since the pandemic started, but at the end of the day, he calculated the most effective way to navigate this dying and fragmented world was on foot.

A bicycle might be easier and faster, especially with gear to carry. But he'd never been a cyclist. He didn't have the balance for it. Things happened too fast on the bike, and he was afraid he wouldn't be able to react in time. At his age, a crash meant near-certain injury—and in this new, chaotic world, a broken clavicle could be a death sentence.

He wondered if some of those trail friends were still out there in the mountains running day and night, oblivious to the disease that had ravaged humanity?

Would they pop out of a trailhead some morning and see the destruction and chaos? What would that be like?

They'd probably just smile and keep running, like he did.

He smiled now as the road ran through a stand of poplars. The sun filtered through the tree trunks and reflected up off the litter of freshly fallen yellow leaves. He paused to take a drink from one of the bottles he carried.

"Hold up, Bill. Let's get a drink."

The big dog circled back and sat at his feet. The old man detached the collapsible bowl from his pack and squirted some water into it.

He sat on his haunches and watched as Bill lapped at the water. He looked down and considered his feet. The dirty big toes sticking out from the homemade sandals he was wearing.

It was a trick he had learned from some Central Americans on the trail circuit. Make your own sandals and never have to buy running shoes again. Something else useful for the apocalypse.

The strap on these sandals was wearing a bit thin. He'd have to craft another pair soon.

There were thick shiny callouses where the rubber straps ground against his feet, day in and day out.

He smiled at them and said to the dog, "I'll be long gone before we run out of tires to salvage for sandals."

These days he ran in a sturdy pair of cutoff camo shorts that he had commandeered from the Corporal's house, fashioned just above the knees. A machete was holstered at one hip, a hunting knife at the other.

A rough work shirt covered by a multi-pocketed vest rode on his torso. His crossbow was slung on top of a light pack.

His kit for the apocalypse hadn't changed much from his trail days and had gotten him this far. He had no need for guns or any other complexities that would just slow him down.

He felt the fading bruise on his side and shifted his pack where a heavy lump was digging into his spine. He flashed back to the guns at the Corporal's house. He remembered the wild pig episode and thought, *maybe guns are good for something, but I'm going to stick with what I know for now...mobility over firepower...*

He figured it was eight-plus weeks after the big die-off.

The virus didn't do all the work. The collapse of government and infrastructure and a certain laissez-faire, every man-for-himself bedlam did the rest.

It took maybe two to three weeks for it all to fall in on itself like a worm-ridden old shack.

Based on what he saw of the mortality rates, he deduced that the virus had probably reduced the world population by more than ninety percent. Maybe there were variances in different localities, but he figured, overall, they were probably back to Iron Age population levels.

What happened now? What happened next? Was there a chance for recovery? For the cultural and governmental infrastructure to return?

Maybe the representatives of a recently defunct government would claw back control. There *might* be a government somewhere. Squirreled away in a bunker. Waiting for their chance to emerge and take back control of taxes and nuclear bombs.

Probably not.

More likely civilization would recover the same way it always had when empires fell.

Small bands and communities would start to pop up again. Humans, as they do, would huddle together as family groups on fortified farms.

As he thought about it, it *was* quite a bit like Iron Age hill forts. Maybe all that reading of history he had done in his life would come in handy in this new world.

There might be herd immunity now, for those that survived. But, that didn't mean the virus would just disappear. Unless that immunity was somehow passed from mothers to offspring with no decay the population would take generations to recover.

If it ever did.

As a doctor, or rather an ex-doctor, his mind logically worked through the likely scenarios.

For a few generations, the young would die off at alarmingly high rates as the human body figured out a way to deal with this plague like it had figured out how to deal with all the others that came before.

If they made it through this bottleneck, these communities would begin to aggregate as they always did.

And the cycle would begin anew.

Local power centers would pop up.

Family groups would expand into tribes.

Leaders would begin to emerge.

Tribes would produce warlords.

Warlords would evolve into lords.

Lords would turn into kings.

History would repeat itself ad nauseum until an asteroid showed up or the sun burned out.

His GPS stopped working. Not because the satellites stopped but because the battery died, and he couldn't recharge it.

The satellites were still up there somewhere, circling the old Mother Earth in standard orbits, pinging relentlessly to a world that didn't hear them anymore.

His solar charger had broken.

He was pretty sure there was no longer an army of Chinese factory workers to make him a new one, or an internet company to deliver it if they did.

Where were all those great container ships now? Washed up on derelict beaches like miserable old sea monsters?

He was making his way generally west. He moved along the back roads across the Appalachians into Tennessee.

He just kept moving.

He stayed away from cities, with their armies of black rats, corpses, and miasmas.

He kept moving. As his trail friends used to say, "Relentless forward motion".

It kept the ghosts at bay.

***

A rock outcropping ran along one side of the gravel road. A common formation in this part of the world. Great grey shards of sedimentary rock pushed up by continental drift. Jumbles of boulders in some places and sheer rock shelves in others.

They ranged in height from a few feet tall to a couple hundred. They peeked out from under wooded hills and dripped water from their mossy hides. It was an imposing and dark place. The old man imagined the dens of bears or abandoned mine shafts.

A slow, late-summer stream ran along the other side of the road, sometimes petering out into swampy ground, sometimes gouging away at the road itself from recent high-water events.

The old man kept a wary eye on the rock shelf as he ran along. If there was trouble, it would come from that side. Bill the Dog kept his nose in the air as well, occasionally glancing back at the old man for guidance.

The road rose in a steep grade cut into the cliffs. A rusted guardrail ran along the downhill side. The old man breathed hard working his way up the hill.

Then, Bill the Dog lifted his head and stopped, acting out the alert message that the old man was becoming attuned to.

The old man stopped too.

"What is it, Bill?" he asked in a conspiratorial whisper. "Another house? A body?"

The big dog did not say but dipped his head in the direction that they were traveling with a worried look.

"OK, big guy. I get it. *Something* is up ahead? Let's stay quiet and low until we see what we're dealing with."

The old man moved to the side of the road and advanced in a crouch, Bill the Dog beside him silent and cautious.

There was a wide bend in the road, and they would need to move a few yards before they could see around it.

As they inched around the corner, a vehicle came into view. They stopped moving and settled in, to assess the situation.

The old man signaled to Bill to hold and lowered into a thoughtful squat.

He couldn't make out clearly what it was. He fished into a vest pocket and carefully unwrapped a pair of eyeglasses.

They said age brought wisdom. But being old *was not* a great gift in the apocalypse. He didn't need glasses for reading or walking around but could use a bit of help for clarity at a distance.

He made a mental note to keep his eyes open for a pair of binoculars.

A pickup truck was pulled off to the side. It didn't look like it had moved recently.

Off the road, beyond the derelict truck, there seemed to be something in the brush. He could make out flashes of blue. It was the ubiquitous sky blue of tarps.

He scratched his scraggly beard, and dust fell from his sun-browned, wind-burned face. He looked at Bill and said "Well, let's go see what we have. Stay close."

Straightening up with effort, the old man began to slowly close the distance. Bill followed on the old man's heel, cautious and alert.

On closer inspection, the truck was covered in muddy dust and looked like it hadn't moved in a long time. One door was canted open, and the cabin floor was full of leaves. The door had the crest and name of a university on it. There were assorted papers strewn about and a muddy hard hat behind the seat.

The ground around had no signs of foot traffic. There didn't seem to be any recent activity here, which the old man thought was a good thing. He didn't need any more crazies in his life right now.

He peered over the truck hood towards where he had glimpsed the tarps in by the cliff.

Probably another derelict campsite. There were lots of them in the woods from when the population fled the cities in the early days. He sniffed at the air and did not smell anything that would betray the living or the dead.

The old man slowly moved away from the road, towards the cliff, staying out of sight, checking for any signs of people, and listening for activity as he went. Bill dutifully followed along, intensely focused.

"What are you worried about dog?" The old man asked conversationally in a low voice, "Doesn't look like anyone has been here for a while..."

Still, the old man stayed alert. If there was trouble, he could make a break for it or fight, and he had the dog. That might make people think twice about messing with him.

The path led to an open area littered with blown tarps in heaps and a couple of those pop-up tents, like the kids would use at soccer when it rained.

It wasn't a campsite. It was something else.

Then something in his pattern-matching brain recognized the setup. Next to a torn and crumpled pop-up tent, he saw something he recognized.

A screening table. A pile of dirt. Buckets. He had seen versions of this in the Sudan at a site where a team was looking for Nubian artifacts.

This was some sort of archeological dig!

Not a big one. Probably a local university project, which would explain the truck.

The rock shelter, the screening table for sifting out artifacts from the soil, it all made sense.

Had to be.

That fitting of all the pieces together into a narrative made the old man happy. It always made him happy when his experience and his brain solved a puzzle like this.

He had always been fascinated by archeology. The classical Egyptians, Greeks, and Romans.

The irony that two thousand years from now, some future archeologists might be wondering what caused modern civilization to collapse, did occur to the old man.

He made his way cautiously to the edge of the cliff and peeked over. Below was the dig site. There was a wooden ladder affixed to the cliffside that led down. There was a pulley system to haul the buckets up to be screened.

He was very curious. He wanted to climb down and check it out.

He hesitated. Was it safe? Should he really be climbing up and down ladders after all he'd been through? Or was he tempting fate, risking his life even, for what? Curiosity?

But, not seeing any recent signs of activity, he concluded the place was abandoned, probably early on, when the first warnings came out.

He dropped his pack and tested the ladder for soundness.

Bill the Dog, already agitated by this strange place, acted like he didn't want the old man to climb down. Bill let out short barks and crouched, staring at the old man as if the old man was being a stupid child.

"Jeez dog! What's up your ass?" The old man scolded, looking around. "There's no one here! It'll be ok. I'll be right back. You stay!"

He was curious. He was a fan of history and always liked archeology.

The old man tested the ladder again, then began to slowly climb down to the dig site.

The old man finished descending and looked around. It was an open plateau that jutted out of the cliff. The view was great. Forested hills rolled out into the horizon, dotted here and there with farms and split occasionally by the black ribbon of a road.

He could imagine native Americans gathered here in this defensible place cooking venison over a warm fire.

He saw that over against the cliff face, under the ledge was the dig pit. It was a natural rock shelter and probably had been home to generations of history.

This would be the heart of the excavation.

Plastic buckets, tarps, and a large, meticulously dug deep trench.

He squatted at the edge of the trench, peering down.

The walls were tagged with little flags and the floor was marked off with a string grid.

The pit was already starting to fill up with leaves - nature ever grinding away at the works of man.

Bill the Dog barked from above and the old man turned to look up.

Suddenly, there was a flash in his peripheral view. Something hit him from the side with a hard shove. He was falling. The impact, a bright flash of pain, and he lost consciousness.

***

When he came back to the light, he was groggy and confused.

The old man rolled over onto his back, propped himself up against the pit wall. He fought an urge to panic.

He felt around, moved, and flexed different parts of his body, testing. Nothing was broken. Just had the wind knocked out of him. Would be sore later.

He was at the bottom of the pit. It was about eight feet deep with vertical walls.

He could climb out easily enough by digging hand and foot holds in the corner.

But that wasn't the issue.

The issue was the silhouette of a woman crouched at the rim, in the dying sunlight, watching him.

Chapter Eighteen - Infected

The old man pushed himself to a sitting position, his back against the far wall of the pit. He reflexively clutched at his shoulder and massaged the side that had taken the brunt of the impact. He could hear the steady drip of water falling from the cliff face and the wind pushing dead leaves around above.

In the background, the dog barked in a way that was somewhere between questioning and threatening.

He slowly lifted his gaze to the surface level to assess the *real* enigma: the woman.

The woman who had shoved him into the pit was silhouetted against the low winter sky.

She squatted at the edge, looking at him.

The old man instinctively reached for his crossbow before realizing it was with his pack on the bluff above.

He cursed himself for being incautious. For leaving his pack with his weapons behind to climb down here. For not keeping the dog with him.

The dog continued to make noise, and the old man wondered if Bill might try to jump down into the dig site. It was a long drop. The dog might be frantic enough to do it and break its leg. What was worse, if the dog did manage to get down here safely, this woman might hurt him. Or he might hurt her. Either way, it would be a situation out of the old man's control and that would not be good.

'Wait a second,' he thought, *'Now I care about the dog? Now I care about this woman? Why?'* He searched his mind for the source of this sudden and unexpected empathy.

The irony of it struck him hard. He had wanted to be alone. He had tried to push the dog away and refuse the company, but now, he was worried about him? He didn't even know who this woman was but now, he was concerned about her wellbeing too?

What the hell was going on?

The tricksy world was poking at him again.

He was trapped at the bottom of a dig pit at the mercy of this woman. His carelessness might be his undoing. He couldn't expect second chances in this unraveling world.

This might be it. The end of the line. *'Fair enough,* he thought, *'I'll end up with the rest of the artifacts down here for future archeologists to puzzle over. A good an end as any...'*

To his own amazement, he realized he really didn't want to just roll over and die right now. He had things to do. He had the dog and wanted to find Paul.

As he assessed the apparition above him, she appeared more thoughtful than actively hostile.

Like she was considering him. Assessing him. Weighing him. He wondered which way the scales were tipping.

Maybe he could talk to her. Work something out. Maybe they could, *God help him*, help each other?

Her silhouette couldn't hide the fact that she was a solid, and athletically built woman. She didn't look soft like many of his former patients in the city ...back when he had patients. He could see the flex of muscle in her thighs and calves as she squatted and noted the defined muscles of her shoulders.

She looked like someone who worked out and stayed fit. Strong but not bulky. And not overly sleek like those urban professionals whose schedules were fixed around cappuccinos, spin classes, and eating disorders.

In a different setting, he might have thought her attractive. But age and circumstance pushed these thoughts from his mind.

She had her shoulder-length brown hair pulled back into a business-like ponytail. The dirt and grime of the apocalypse was on her. Like it was on everyone now. No one woke up to a hot shower anymore.

He really missed hot showers.

To the old man, it seemed a great irony. Just when he was starting to consider living again. Had even made friends with a dog. Here he was. In the woods. In an archeological dig. In a hole. '*I guess I'm the fossil now,*' he thought to himself.

What was it that one of his buddies had always said in situations like this?

'God certainly has a sense of humor.'

He surveyed the dark pit and thought, '*A man should never have to see his own grave.*' He peered up at the woman silhouetted at the hole's lip.

"Hello?" he offered, tentatively.

There was no response.

The old man slowly and cautiously gathered himself. He stood up, testing his muscles and bones in the process. At least nothing felt broken.

The woman tensed, continued to eye him closely, and shifted her weight like a big cat readying to pounce.

He eased back against the wall of the pit, rubbed his sore shoulder, and considered her.

***

KJ watched the man she had shoved into the pit and considered one thing, because there was really only one thing that mattered in this particular situation.

Was he a threat? Would she...*should she*...need to kill this man?

It had been almost ten days since her encounter with Karl at the camper. She had been overconfident then and it had almost cost her.

She had found enough food and water to survive but she was injured, and that made this man a risk. She wasn't at her best. She had been hiding here hoping to heal.

People were different now, unhinged from civil actions and attitudes. There was no rule of law. She was her own law now.

She assessed the man in the pit. He was not physically big, probably a couple of inches shorter than she was, thin and wiry. He didn't look like a threat, but you never knew. The apocalypse could have made him crazy...or unlocked his existing crazy.

She was learning that *Crazy* beat *Size* in the apocalypse. And *Crazy* didn't follow any rules.

The dig site had been her hiding place for a few days. But her foot wasn't getting better. Her toe was swollen and red and pus had started to ooze from under the nail. She couldn't even get the shoe back on. It hurt like hell to walk on it. She was considering trying to relieve the pressure by drilling a hole in the nail with her knife, but that might just make it worse.

The irony wasn't lost on her that she hurt herself kicking that piece of shit Karl. It would be a pyrrhic victory if she won the fight but lost her foot or died out here in the woods from a blood infection.

She refocused on the matter at hand. What to do with this man?

She was almost willing to believe that not *everyone* was a threat, but that had not been her experience so far. Before the apocalypse, you could give someone the benefit of the doubt. Since the apocalypse, she was learning to *trust no one.*

"What now?" The voice of the man in the pit brought her back to reality. He sounded calm. He wasn't being aggressive. Of course, he was at a significant disadvantage. But not sounding unhinged was a start.

She did not respond.

"Do you want something?" He continued.

Still, she did not respond.

She had a decision to make. She had to decide how to engage. *"Let's start with a bit of silence and see how he reacts..."* She thought. She knew from her deposition experience that silence was a powerful tool. It was a way to control interactions if used correctly. People hated silence. It made them uncomfortable. They usually filled it with something they later wished they hadn't.

***

The old man considered the woman again.

She wasn't talking. Was there something wrong with her?

His brain flashed an image from an old book or play he had read...what was it? Euripides? Homer? Shakespeare? He forgot the book but recalled the image of a warrior queen. The thought made him smile and he addressed the woman again.

He realized he had nothing to lose at this point, except, of course, his life, but he had come to grips with that eventuality already in his travels.

"I'll just call you *Hippolyta*." He paused, slightly impressed with himself. "Do you know who that was?"

She didn't answer.

"Queen of the Amazons," he pronounced rather grandly. He grinned up at her, waiting for a response.

If he was going to get snuffed out in a hole, in the dirt, he might as well say what he was thinking.

It fit, he thought, she *was* Amazonian in nature and form. She was fit, muscular, and athletic under the crust of grime that they all wore now.

Amazonian.

Martial and intimidating in her demeanor.

She had a hard look about her. No-nonsense. Used to getting her way.

Amazonian.

Her feet were just above his eye-level now. Curiously, one foot displayed a dirty sock and the other was bare. The bare foot was dirty brown like worn leather and the big toe didn't look good.

***

Janet considered this new line of conversation about Amazons that the man offered and thought, '*Was this a normal thing to say?*'

He called her the 'Queen of the Amazons'. That was rich. Some Queen she was. '*Currently, The Queen is probably dying of an infection and in need of help.*'

"Are you alone?" She asked.

"Yes and no." He paused and smiled. "That barking you hear is a friend of mine. He's a very loyal dog, and I don't know why, but he likes me." The old man in the hole looked at her like he was considering how much to share. "I don't think he'd hurt you unprovoked, but you should probably be careful. You don't want to tangle with him."

She raised her eyes and glanced up over her shoulder towards the cliff edge where the dog barked incessantly.

She looked back at the man, shifted her weight, and stared down with a heavy look of malice.

"I could kill you in that hole and take my chances."

***

The old man looked at the ground and thought about how to respond.

"I suppose you could," he finally concluded with an exhale. "Be like shooting fish in a barrel. Although, that probably isn't your biggest problem right now. You see, I'm a doctor; a vascular surgeon, as it turns out."

Her eyes widened a bit.

He saw her reaction and smiled inwardly at the power of that statement. How people, on discovering you were a doctor treated you differently, like you had some sort of life-over-death superhero powers.

He pressed his advantage.

He smiled, nodded, and kept speaking in that low, soothing doctor's voice he had crafted through years of practice. He called it his '*trust voice*'. "That toe is infected. Without treatment, you risk gangrene. It's not going to get better by itself."

She glanced down at the toe and back at him.

"Kicked something," she said, without further explanation.

He let that go for now and returned to his point. "Do you know how it ends for you?" he asked, warming to his topic. "Untreated, it will spread to the foot, the leg, and eventually you'll die of sepsis. It's not pretty. *Although* you might be able to amputate your own foot, if that sounds like fun to you."

He paused for dramatic effect, maybe a bit too long, and spread his arms with his hands up like a statue of Jesus.

"So, I guess you have a choice." He paused again for effect. "You can be attacked by a big dog and die a horrible death in a couple of weeks." He raised one hand, looked at it as if it held that choice, and smiled again. "Or," raising the other hand, "I can come up there and fix that for you."

Then he added, "...and I'll make you a new pair of sandals in the bargain. What's it going to be?"

***

Janet watched him give his pitch. She had seen so many of these sanctimonious bastards give pitches – trying to talk their way out of accountability in the courtroom, thinking they knew more than their patients.

She could rid the world of one more cockroach right here, right now.

Make the world a better place.

But wasn't that what they always said about *lawyers*? That the world would be better off without them?

That world was gone. She wasn't a lawyer anymore; she was a survivor.

He sounded like a doctor. What he said was true. She'd worked on enough liability cases to know how people died of sepsis. Typically, after some pretentious doctor like this one sewed a surgical instrument up inside them.

The foot *had* been getting worse. There was the pain. But now it was feeling hot and smelled funky. She knew that was not a good sign.

Whether she liked it or not she needed help. To get that help she'd need to relinquish control; to stop being the killer so she could go on living.

She made a decision.

"It's your lucky day," she said, not smiling, but at the same time thinking to herself, *'I'm not going to kill you...not yet...not today...But if you give me a reason I won't hesitate'.*

He shrugged and nodded acceptance. She looked at him hard and long, shook her head, unfolded from her crouch, and reached for the ladder.

She hoped she had made the right decision.

***

Later that day, she lay on an impromptu bench with her foot propped up, while the old-man-who-might-be-a-doctor fussed over it.

"It's not too bad." The old man dropped into a clucking monolog. "I've seen worse. I can drain it, clean it, and wrap it, but we really should get you some antibiotics."

Janet winced as he poked at the toe with a knife.

The old man shrugged. "Sorry, it's going to hurt. Not much I can do about that."

"Are you sure you're a doctor?" Janet grimaced.

The old man looked hurt and solemnly held one hand to his heart and raised the other in a pledge. "Scout's honor."

Bill the Dog lay on the ground next to them, watching and curious of this newcomer. He had greeted her with a few sniffs and had pushed his big head into her lap for some love, wagging that big brush of a tail.

It was anticlimactic after all the noise the dog was making. The old man considered it a good sign. Dogs were usually good judges of character. But then again, he hadn't known this dog for very long either. Maybe the dog just liked anyone who didn't immediately threaten him.

The old man had his back to her now as he worked on the toenail. "You might want to grab hold of something," he suggested. "I've got to get under the nail, and this is going to hurt like hell."

Janett looked around for something. She grabbed a grapefruit-sized, jagged rock in one hand and squeezed it hard. She gritted her teeth and tried not to scream.

Her whole body tensed as the pain shot through her like a searing hot metal shard. What the hell was he doing? What kind of butcher had she let at her toe? She considered the jagged rock in her hand and the back of the old man's head.

The Dog tensed forward from his crouch a couple of inches and gave a preemptive low growl.

The old man looked at the dog and then in the direction of the dog's attention.

He frowned. "Almost done. You're doing great. Hang in there. Almost done." The old man reached out a hand and gently patted her forearm. It was meant to be a comforting gesture. She stiffened and pulled back from his touch. He nodded, smiled weakly, and turned back to the toe.

Janet rolled up her shirt, stuck it into her mouth, clamped down, and nodded back at him in confirmation.

***

After he was done, he explained it to her.

He had cleaned the infection as much as he could, spritzed the area with antiseptic spray, and wrapped it with clean bandages from the small camping med kit he had. He finished the job with some duct tape. That would make a solid protection around the wound.

He declared officiously that there was a chance it might heal on its own if it could be kept clean and she stayed off it.

KJ allowed a grim smile at the duct tape, remembering Karl trussed up in the dirt.

The old man considered his work and said to her, "Not emergency room standards, but it'll do for a field wrap." He concluded, "OK, we're all done for now. We're going to have to keep it clean. You probably won't be able to walk much for a while." He looked at her. "We really should get you some antibiotics."

'We', Janet considered silently. *Hadn't she just recently been considering killing this man? And now he's talking like they were some sort of team?*

"And where do *we* find those?" she asked, speaking slowly and clearly, drawing out the *'we'* without emotion.

"I don't know," he admitted. "I suppose we're just going to keep a look out and check any buildings we come across. See what we can find. A better question is, how are you going to travel? Any chance the truck would start?"

She shook her head. "No. I checked it. It's dead. If it would start, it probably wouldn't be here."

"Huh, well that's a problem."

***

He didn't know why, but this woman felt familiar. Had he known her in another life? Had they met before? She resembled one of his nieces maybe. His ex's sister's kid?

Maybe it wasn't the woman who was familiar. Maybe it was the interaction.

He had wanted to stay alone out here, had preferred being alone, had finally gotten used to being alone. Now he had a dog and...*this woman*.

God help him, but the company of another human made him feel better. Being able to help her, to practice his art, had touched him with a familiarity of purpose that made him feel more alive.

More alive than he'd felt in months. Not such a bad thing to feel in the apocalypse.

***

Her toe had morphed from searing pain to a dull throb after the old man wrapped it. He seemed to have done something positive. He probably *was* a doctor. She still didn't trust him. She still sensed something *off* in him. She could—she *would* still take his life if she had to.

But it seemed like she'd be less-than-mobile for the foreseeable future. He and the dog, if they could be trusted, could help her get past this point of vulnerability. After that, she would reassess his usefulness and their arrangement.

'*Call it a 'truce' then,'* she thought. She would suffer his presence but keep her guard up. Treat it as a probationary period.

"How long before I can walk on this?" Janet asked, looking at the foot like it was an offensive piece of rotten fruit.

"Well, if you can keep it clean, and the infection goes down, maybe a week."

"I can't stay here for a week." She replied.

"If we could find some antibiotics, it would heal up much faster. But we need to be mobile to look for them." The old man shrugged.

"Couldn't we improvise some sort of litter?" she asked, "There is some worksite equipment in the back over there. Maybe there is something you could cannibalize?"

The use of the word *'cannibalize'* seemed to throw him for a second. Poor choice of words on her part. She had no doubt that somewhere, probably not too far away, that term might be far too accurate.

He saved her from the awkward moment by asking, "You mean MacGyver something to transport the patient?" He considered the concept for a moment. "Yeah, I see what you mean, that might work."

He began to smile again. It looked to her like the suggestion had taken root and was flowering in his imagination. He turned and wandered into the dig site with a renewed purpose.

Chapter Nineteen - Prey

It was a bumpy and uncomfortable ride. The old man chittered on happily behind her like old people...or *senile* people do.

Like when your mom or grandma keeps an entire conversation going regardless of whether you are even listening.

Those interminable phone calls Janet used to dread and avoid, droning on and on about the flotsam and jetsam of an old person's life, only to surface from the lily pads every once in a while, to ask some prying or unanswerable... *personal* question.

Janet felt a momentary pang of sadness.

Maybe she should have taken the time to talk – *to listen* – when she had the chance.

Before her mom and everyone she knew was taken by the apocalypse.

The old man was on a long soliloquy about the impact of humanity on the natural flow of water and how that was now being reversed, as rivers and streams were allowed to make up their own minds.

He seamlessly transitioned into a monologue on how the failing infrastructure was a risk for them and how they should avoid cities to survive.

'At least', she thought with relief, *'My part in this conversation is limited to an occasional exasperated sigh'.*

She did not think he was dangerous. Not directly dangerous to her, anyhow. She wasn't sure if he was *'all there'* or not. But these days, they *all* suffered from different degrees of damage. Their minds were making up new playbooks as they went along.

She'd keep an eye on him and keep her guard up.

She wasn't even quite sure of *her own* sanity, but, like everything else, she had buried those concerns in the business of day-to-day survival.

The old man had rigged up this contrived cart from spare parts at the dig site. Some wheels and other bits and pieces.

He had done this mechanical work after cleaning her infected toe and treating it as best as he could. The verdict on the toe still wasn't clear. He said he didn't know if he'd have to go in and take a more aggressive approach, but he recommended giving it a chance to heal, to avoid losing the offending digit.

They'd wait and see. She couldn't walk, but thought it was a good idea to keep moving. He agreed. He thought it best to see if they could find some antibiotics. At first, he suggested that he go ahead and scout while she stayed and healed. He said he'd come back when he found something.

Janet had told him in no uncertain terms that she did not approve of that plan. If he was going, she would go with him. At least until she could walk. She didn't trust him to come back and didn't want to be left, virtually helpless, at the dig site.

After some argument, he had given in and said, "Well then, I'll have to take you with me."

Once that decision was made, he had bustled around the dig site, cackling to himself and exclaiming, "Dammit Jim, I'm a doctor, not a bicycle mechanic!" KJ gave him a hard look of disapproval. She had no idea what he was on about most of the time.

In the end, he was impressed with himself, having thrown together a makeshift rickshaw of sorts - a wheelbarrow bucket mounted on some lumber framing with a couple of wheels. It was a cramped and uncomfortable conveyance, but it worked.

The wheels were from a discarded and broken cart. The bucket for Janet's conveyance sat between the wheels, positioned in the middle, to spread the weight evenly.

She rode in the bed of the contraption with her feet dangling out the front, sitting on some of the folded-up blue tarps. Two long handles, with a crosspiece wired on for pushing, jutted out the back. He held these while he walked or jogged behind.

Janet had watched him assemble the rickshaw. It took him the better part of two days.

Her foot seemed to be getting better, but it was still sore and swollen. Without antibiotics, there was nothing more he could do, other than keep it clean and change the bandage.

The cartwheels were smaller than bicycle wheels and had solid rubber instead of balloon tires. That made them slower and less responsive to the rough roads, but also meant they didn't need to worry about the tires going flat.

It was awkward and unwieldy to push. Even with his fitness, he couldn't go much faster than a quick walk. But it allowed them to keep moving and they followed the gravel road along the river westward towards the hills.

Bill the Dog jogged out in front of them. He had recently found and rolled in something dead. As a result, he was ostracized from their close company and told to keep his distance. They hoped whatever dead thing he had rolled in was an animal.

Then, in his vanguard position out front, Bill froze.

KJ was the first to see him stop and come to an alert. Then she saw something else. Four large, unusual animals standing on the road ahead.

Bill looked back at them from his alert with a questioning glance, like he was asking "What do you want me to do?"

The old man stopped the cart, squinted up the road, and said quietly and firmly, "Leave it!" to the dog.

Bill sat, looking a bit disappointed.

"What the heck are those? Ostriches?" She asked.

The old man pulled the glasses from his vest pocket, unwrapped them from their chamois cloth, and fitted them into place. He peered down the road curiously for a few seconds and corrected her. "Emu. Four Emu. Ostriches are from Africa, Emus are from Australia. There are no large flightless birds in North America. There's the Rhea in South America and of course, the Terror Bird, a nasty bit of work there, but they've been gone for a few million years..."

She looked at him, speechless. She wanted to say, "What the hell are you talking about, you crazy old bastard?" But decided not to waste her breath, as it might encourage him. "OK, Emus, Ostriches...*Big Bird*...you're missing my point. What are they doing here?"

He scratched his beard in thought, bits of dust circled his head like a weird halo.

"Dunno," he finally concluded and looked at her. "What say we find out?" He smiled. "Why don't you stay here, and I'll go see?"

"That's not going to happen," she said with a finality that precluded any argument. She hoisted herself upright and gingerly began moving down the road with the help of an improvised crutch, hop-walking on her good leg.

He shrugged and followed, easily pushing the empty rickshaw.

The Emus were skittish and retreated as KJ, the old man, and Bill approached. All at once, they scattered into the brush. Bill watched their long, loping chicken legs recede with interest, hoping he'd be told to give chase.

Next, there were loud screeches coming from the trees as they continued to move down the road.

KJ glanced at the old man with a questioning look.

He met her look with a puzzled look of his own, like he was trying to remember something that was just out of reach. He said, "Maybe catbirds? There's something familiar about those calls...I've heard them somewhere before."

KJ kept looking at him. "That doesn't sound like any bird I've ever heard...Could it be something out of place like the Emu's?"

"That's it!" The old man raised a finger. "Africa! I've heard those before in Africa! Those are monkey calls!"

Janet gave him another long look. "What? No speech about the North American Monkey...?"

"Humans are the only primates in North America." He said. "But that sounds like a Howler Monkey or maybe a Macaque and they shouldn't be here."

They proceeded slowly up the road, curious and cautious.

Bill stayed close to the edge of the road, head sweeping from side to side, clearly on guard and alert.

Shortly, they came upon an iron pipe gate with a sign that read "Perkins' Animal Park". The words were in a circus font and bracketed by silhouettes of men in cowboy hats.

The old man brightened. "Jackpot! If they've got animals, then they should have a way to treat them. There's a good chance there are antibiotics in there."

KJ held back. "Wait," she said in a tone that made people wait. "What's the plan?"

"Plan? Well, I suppose we go in and look for an admin building with a medical cabinet."

"What about the *animals* in this 'animal' park?" she asked, nodding towards the sign on the gate.

The old man thought about that for a moment. "Well, it looks like someone's been letting them out. I suppose any left in their cages would be mostly dead by now, right? We just take it slow and easy and if we smell trouble, we leg it." He winced a bit, remembering her foot. "I mean there's three of us, we'll scare off anything that's in there. Look, lady, if we find some antibiotics we, can save your foot."

She nodded but looked pensive. As a predator, she was always on the alert for other predators, but how much of a predator was she now?

She could barely walk.

The old man led them, gingerly picking his way with as much stealth as possible down the entranceway to the main park. KJ followed, with Bill flanking out to the side.

Bill was on edge. Up to this point he had been relaxed, almost casual. The old man even managed to practice some commands with him. But now, this was different, Bill was serious, and his training was starting to show through.

He was working.

Passing by the enclosures, they saw that some of the cages were open. Some were still closed with the remains of whatever had been left behind, confined for eternity. The sun was out, and the heat of the day added to the oppressive nature of the place. The smell of rot and death was thick in the air.

They checked a few buildings and to their surprise, there were remains there too. Carcasses.

And not all animals.

It was hard to say exactly what had happened. Everything was in the advanced stages of decomposition or had been partially eaten by scavengers. They looked at each other and shared a new sense of discomfort as their exploration had taken a darker turn.

The first buildings they passed were the customer-facing type; gift shops and food stalls. Junk food wrappers and garbage were spread around by foraging animals.

Towards the back, behind the animal enclosures, was a long, barn-like structure that might be what they were looking for.

As they made their way, they remained on high alert, staying close to the walls and watching Bill for cues.

For his part, Bill was really working now, like this was a familiar activity, searching buildings with the potential of hostile surprises. He would sweep along a building, stop at the corner, listen, look, and make eye contact with the old man before moving forward.

Eventually, they gained the barn-like building and pushed the door open. They stepped into a large, open lobby of sorts. There was a counter with office space behind it, lit by dusty sunlight slanting through the windows of the tall central peak of the structure.

Rough wood barn-board walls held a whiteboard, an institutional clock with its hands frozen from when the power had cut out, and a calendar with an African scene of giraffes on the savannah in the sunset.

The old man told Bill to sit and stay. The dog looked tense. They were still getting to know one another. Their communication and execution had yet to be perfectly synchronized. But Bill took the orders. He dutifully positioned himself just inside the door as a sentry.

KJ and the old man entered.

Behind the counter, there were offices along the northern wall of the building. It got progressively dimmer as they crept towards the back, where the sunlight struggled to reach.

Even in the dull shadows, the old man knew they had found what they were looking for in a darkened room with a smattering of veterinary equipment.

There was a large metal table in the center of the room. The floor was hard with speckled linoleum sloping toward a drain in the corner.

The old man began rummaging through drawers and cabinets, using a hammer he had found to force some of them open. He was squinting at pill bottles in the dim light.

"Dammit!" He cursed under his breath. "Can you read these labels? We're looking for 'Cipro.'" He started to spell it for her but stopped when he noticed her menacing glare.

Then, a low and guttural growl came from the front of the building.

Bill!

KJ and the old man froze.

The old man had heard Bill make that sound before, the day Bill went after the pack of wild pigs. They couldn't see him, but it sounded like he was still at the main door to the building, where the old man had stationed him.

Something was wrong.

Bill's growls grew more focused. They morphed into an angry, warning bark.

Something was out there.

The old man and KJ looked at each other, silently, meeting each other's eyes with a look that exchanged an encyclopedia's volume of critical understanding.

KJ stuffed a couple of pill bottles quickly into a pocket and they began to move towards the door.

As Bill's growls and barks became more aggressive, another low and rumbling groan joined in, a thrum that you felt in your chest as much as heard.

This was the sound of something very large and very near.

The old man hissed the German command for silence to Bill, *"Ruhig!"*

The dog stopped barking, but they could sense his tension and hear the click of his nails on the floor as he shifted.

The old man peered through the small window in the office door and saw what the dog was warning them about.

A large lioness had entered the main building and was coming in their direction.

They were trapped!

As the old man watched, Bill reacted.

He resumed barking aggressively, making a move to attack the lioness that looked to be three times his size. Bill lunged, stepped back, then made a flanking move and zig-zagged by the lion, snapping at its haunches. Bill was trying to distract the predator and draw her away. The lioness appeared surprised and annoyed. She lunged and swiped at him, but he stayed out of reach.

Realizing that the dog was no match for the big cat, the old man shouted through the door, "LEAVE IT!"

Bill halted his dervish-like harassment of the lioness and backed away a few paces, staring at her, hackles raised, growling and baring his teeth. Momentarily, Bill and the lioness circled each other like boxers in a ring.

The lioness stopped and looked towards where the old man's shout had emanated from. She made a huffing sound and slowly turned in the direction of the old man. Maybe she was thinking that she could come back for the dog later; that she had other, easier prey available.

The old man could see that the lioness was starving. As much as the apocalypse had been a seismic shift of survival for the humans, this poor animal was equally traumatized.

Someone had let her out. Maybe one of those crumpled forms they passed.

No more would the trainers show up with fresh meat. She was on her own. What was she capable of now?

KJ and the old man crouched low and stayed quiet, hoping the animal would eventually wander away and they could make their escape. But they could hear the low rumbling groan of the lioness vocalizing outside the office door.

The old man leaned forward from his crouch and eased the door closed as quietly as he could until it latched. He hissed a low whisper, "This isn't going to hold. We have to get out of here!"

KJ had seen the lioness too. She motioned to the old man, pointing to the open rafters of the roof, and climbed with her good foot up onto a counter.

The rumbling growl was just outside the door now.

KJ reached up, grabbed one of the barn rafters, and swung herself up.

"Come on!" she hissed.

The door rattled and there was that huffing, snuffling sound, with more urgency and menace now.

Bill's frantic and harassing barks kept up from further away, adding to the frenzied cacophony.

The old man scrambled up on the counter as well, following KJ's lead. He felt the adrenaline of being hunted.

There was a bang, and the door buckled as the lioness jumped against it.

It wasn't going to last much longer.

This predator was hunting them. Remembering the carnage they had seen as they entered, it became obvious that this big cat had taken all the easy prey. The Emus and some tree-climbing monkeys had escaped.

The lioness had her million years of evolutionary imperatives. Hunting ground-dwelling mammals was one of those. She might be hungry, or even psychotic, or maybe she was enacting some forgotten, simple urge to hunt and kill.

Whatever the case, after the apocalypse, this lioness re-established herself at the top of the local food chain, and she was after them.

The old man stood on the counter and reached but couldn't get enough of a grip to pull himself up to the rafters.

He dangled from the beam, legs slip-scraping against the painted wall.

KJ swore and reached down a long arm. She grabbed him by the back of his shirt and jerked him up just as the hunting lioness broke through the door.

The lioness took two strides and jumped at them, sending bottles, containers, and equipment clattering from the counters.

The two survivors perched, clinging to the roof beams with their hearts racing, breathing hard from the effort of climbing and the shock of becoming prey.

They could smell the pungent odor of the beast as the lioness sat below, staring intently at them, ears back, tail twitching on the floor.

"I guess that's what we get for not paying admission!" The old man gasped.

KJ gave him an evil stare. "We have to get out of here." She nodded towards the vent at the end of the roof. "That way."

The big cat circled below, energy dissipating in frustration, as she watched her prey escape along the rafters to an eave at the western end of the building.

When they got to the far eave, KJ pushed out the aluminum grating and managed with some effort to reach up and pull herself onto the roof. She helped the old man up too.

After the old man and KJ were able to successfully clamber through the vent and up onto the roof *without being eaten*, the lioness left the office and moved outside.

The lioness now sat preening herself on a grassy embankment, watching them on the roof, as if to say, "I've got all the time in the world."

"Well, *that* was something..." the old man mused.

"No shit, Sherlock." KJ gave him a hard look like she wasn't interested in any more words from him.

He swallowed a biblical reference about Samson and Delilah that had popped into his mind.

KJ spat in the direction of the lioness and stretched out on her back to look at the hazy southern sun.

And there they sat, not knowing what to do. They had abandoned their packs and weapons in their harried escape.

It was quite a scene.

Cicadas squeaked their lazy violins. Osprey rode thermals over the river looking for fish.

And two lost primates perched precariously on a barn roof.

Chapter Twenty - The Shot

What runs through the mind of a dog?

Not just a dog, but a marine and a veteran.

Bill was quiet now, and alert. His pack was safe. He could see them on the roof of the building, but the large cat was waiting and watching them from below.

The pack was his duty. Bill protected the pack. He would fight, and even die, for his pack.

He held, out of reach of the cat, waiting. It was hot. He was thirsty and hungry.

But he would wait. Until his new man said otherwise. Until the pack was safe.

The new man commanded Bill less than his previous partner, the soldier, had. The new man gave commands but seemed hesitant, unsure. That worried Bill and diminished his confidence.

Bill thought the woman acted more like a pack leader.

They were his pack now. And for Bill the Dog, there was only now. There was only ever the mission.

Bill could fight. Bill could distract and harass. Bill could run.

Bill would do whatever it took to protect the pack.

Bill sniffed the air. There were so many smells in this place.

The smells of animals.

The smell of those big birds that crossed the road.

The sharp smell of rancid meat, rotting trash, and waste.

The smell of death.

The musky ammonia reek of a cat.

There were many smells in this place, but Bill would not be distracted by them.

He would wait. He would watch. That was his job.

He waited for a signal.

The large cat was at rest on the grass, and Bill moved to the edge of the open ground.

The old man saw Bill and made eye contact. Bill accepted the recognition.

He would watch now and wait for a command.

Wait for the right time. To do his duty. To protect the pack.

***

The old man felt the hot asphalt grit of the roofing shingles burning into his backside as he hunched forward with his hands holding his knees.

He alternatively watched the lioness preen herself and glanced at KJ, who lay on her back beside him. She had one arm thrown over her eyes, forearm blocking the sun; the hand of that arm was reflexively clenching and unclenching in troubled thought.

He straightened and looked around, gathering as much information as he could from the view. They were a couple hundred yards from the gravel road. The hills sloped up behind the farm in dense thickets behind a tall fence.

He looked at the woman lying there, and thought to himself, *'Here's another one of those leadership moments.'* He had learned through his life that people naturally turned to him and expected him to lead, to decide, to choose a way forward.

At first, he'd recoiled from it. Who was he to decide the fate of others? He tried to collaborate, to find consensus, and to make decisions as a team.

But people hated that. For the most part, people were sheep. They looked for strength and wanted to be led.

Now he saw it here with this woman. As capable as she was. She just saved his life, in fact! She needed him to lead.

He thought he knew what she was thinking.

She was waiting for him to come up with a plan. To set the tone. To save the day. That's the way it had always been for him. Part of why he'd given up on the world. Why he would rather wander the apocalypse alone – like the anti-hero loner of some fictional epic?

Even before the apocalypse, he had turned away from the world in part because he didn't want to be responsible for other people's fates. He had tried being the one responsible. He had been *that man*, and he didn't want to be that man again.

He looked at her. He knew what she was thinking.

***

KJ lay on her back, head resting on the angle of the roof peak, one arm covering her eyes, and thought through her options.

Another crappy situation, she thought. *Like so many others.*

This world was just a constant parade of crappy situations, and crappy, horrible choices.

God help her, she was starting to get used to it. It was becoming a mental game. Like she was on some sort of horrific game show. She could almost hear the game show host's voice:

"Today's challenge is a ruthless, psychotic lioness bent on securing its next meal. How will she get out of this one? Will she? Or will the game win this time?"

Sigh.

Occam's Razor popped into her mind: *The simplest solution that presents itself is usually the best one.* She was stuck on a roof because of a lioness. The simplest solution would be to push this old man, this cackling idiot, off the roof and use the distraction to move on down the road.

The idea had merit. In fact, on a different day, the lioness would be chewing on the old bugger by now, and KJ would be carrying her self-preservation off into the sunset.

But there was her foot to consider.

She had the antibiotics in her pocket, but would they even work?

She couldn't expect to run. And what about the dog? She supposed the dog would go down fighting trying to save the old man.

It all made option A - the 'sh*ove the old man off the roof'* plan a bit less probable.

It wasn't clear whether the foot was healing or whether it would need more work. As nutty as this guy was, he had demonstrated some medical skills.

The logic gears and probability trees in her brain ground to a halt.

She still needed him...for now.

She sat up, stretched her long arms over her head, interlocked her fingers, and leaned from one side to the other like a sleepy, dangerous cat.

The old man watched her as she shifted her weight and stretched her long, strong frame.

He looked like he was waiting for something.

She turned to him and locked eyes. "What're you looking at?" She asked.

He held her gaze and didn't flinch. "I'm looking at you." He pressed the conversation forward. "Ready to figure out how we get off this roof and get on with our lives without becoming cat scat?"

She smiled. He was trying to be the Man. It was predictable. "OK, Gramps, I'll bite. Whatcha got? Can we kill it?"

The old man stared out into a point in space like he was imagining something and began presenting what he had already thought through in anticipation of this.

"Well, thinking it through, we might be able to distract it and make a run for it, but with you being hobbled, that's probably too risky of a proposition." He continued. "We're not in a great position up on this roof. On one hand, I don't think that cat can get up here, but, on the other, we don't have food or water. Maybe we could get to one of the other buildings and barricade ourselves in, maybe find some weapons."

"What about your dog?" She asked. KJ gestured at the dog who sat at the edge of the clearing watching. "Or your crossbow?" The old man had left his pack down below when they had to scramble out of harm's way.

"I thought about that. Bill would be a gamer, certainly, but even a good-sized dog like Bill versus a three-hundred-pound lion wouldn't end well for the dog. And even if I could get to my gear, I've only got a couple of bolts. The crossbow probably isn't strong enough to kill it. I'd rather find a way out of this that doesn't involve any of us getting killed… even the lioness."

KJ shook her head and said sarcastically, "So you're saying we can't get away, we can't fight it, *and* we can't kill it?"

The old man ignored her and continued, "Hey, have you looked at her?" He gestured to the dozing cat. "She's not healthy. She's starving. She's unexpectedly found herself back on top of the food chain. It's not a bad thing to have an apex predator population hanging around to keep the wild pigs in line. There was a robust mountain lion population here before people showed up. Why kill her if we don't have to? Who are we to decide what gets to live in the apocalypse?"

KJ shook her head again. "I'm stuck on a roof in the apocalypse with a nutjob-pacifist-environmentalist."

She turned and spat at the lion. The predator raised its big head and gave her a disinterested look. "Yeah, that's right!" She said to it and spat again.

"I could kill it with the jawbone of an ass," the old man said, unable to suppress the biblical reference.

"*You're* an ass." She countered. "And your jawbone has been killing me all day with your yappin'."

The old man smiled at this. He squeezed his knees in tighter and turned away so she wouldn't notice.

***

Here he was again in another bad situation. It seemed like the world was just a pinball machine of bad situations now. But at least, he had company.

And he was beginning to think he liked that.

He turned his eyes to the lioness once again. He thought about the wild animal shows he used to watch as a kid.

He had another idea.

"I think I might have something we could try," he said.

"Do tell."

"If you owned a wild animal farm, wouldn't you have a way to control violent animals and keep them from escaping?"

"A big gun?" she replied, deadpan.

"You're close," he nodded. "What other kind of gun? Think about it. Did you ever watch Mutual of Omaha Wild Kingdom? No, of course not—you're too young." He shook his head. "OK, let's go at it this way... In any wildlife show, how do they capture the wild animal to put a tracking tag on it or something?"

She focused and he saw it dawn on her. "Tranquilizer. They hit them with a tranquilizer dart."

"Right. And I bet there's one of those in the office below somewhere. I saw a bottle of Ketamine in one of the locked cabinets that we went through."

"So, we get that, shoot the lioness and move on?"

"It won't be that simple, but, yeah, basically. The gun is going to be in a case of some sort that has what looks like a long-barreled pistol in it, with some of those syringes with the feathers on the end."

He looked at her.

A moment passed.

"You want me to swing back in there and get it."

"Well, yeah. You've got the proven ability to monkey in and out. I can keep the lioness busy and distracted and be your lookout."

"Wow." She shook her head, "Send the girl with the bad foot to do the dirty work."

The old man grinned and shrugged.

***

The old man jumped up and down on the roof, waved his arms, and shouted at the lioness while KJ climbed back into the office to look for the dart gun.

It really wasn't easy. She had to make multiple trips through the vent, across the rafters, and back into the veterinary area.

Each time, she returned with an item she would hand it up to the old man, who would inspect in turn it and tell her what else to look for.

She was eventually able to locate the tranquilizer gun case in a locked cabinet on the wall that she bashed open with a fire extinguisher.

At one point, the old man had to scramble and yell to KJ to move it because the lioness had shifted its attention and was moving in her direction.

As if on cue, Bill the Dog started barking. Bill had recognized the old man's signal and was helping to distract the lion. Bill kept a safe distance from the large cat, but also kept the lion's attention away from KJ.

Bill bought them the time they needed.

After what felt like an eternity but was probably only the better part of an hour, they had the case open, and all the pieces laid out on the roof.

Between the two of them, they were able to figure out the mechanics of the air gun. The old man filled the pressure syringes with what he hoped was the right dosage. KJ inserted a fresh CO_2 cartridge.

There were four air-worthy syringes if the CO_2 cartridges were still good.

"OK – let's do this. We've got four shots," the man said, shifting to a position at the edge of the roof.

He whistled loudly. "Bill, leave it!" He hollered. "Hold!"

Bill cocked his head, looked up at the old man, and went silent.

It wasn't long before the lioness returned her attention to its prey on the roof. She paced the ground in front of them.

KJ watched the old man, doubtfully.

He sat on the roof edge with his feet braced against the gutter and sighted the air gun at the lion. She was sitting in the dirt maybe twenty five feet away, gazing at him. He squinted along the gun barrel and focused for a long few seconds, closing one eye.

He inhaled, held his breath, and squeezed the trigger. There was a popping sound and a puff of dust about three feet to the left of the lioness as the needle skittered in the dirt.

"Damnit!" the old man cursed.

"That wasn't even close," KJ said.

The old man reloaded the gun and resumed his focus with even more intensity.

Another pop and another puff of dust, this time two feet to the right of the lioness who watched the syringe bounce with interest. The big cat got up, sauntered over to where the syringe came to a stop, and sniffed it.

"Two left," the old man said, trying to sound confident as he reloaded the gun.

"Give me that!" KJ said. "You're useless. I'm surprised you haven't shot yourself with that crossbow of yours."

The old man sheepishly handed the gun over.

The lioness had lost interest in the syringe and was now standing facing them. KJ brought the gun level and sighted it.

Again, there was the pop of the gun and another puff of dust, but this time between the lioness's legs and it jumped out of the way, startled and annoyed.

"Reload it," KJ said grimly, handing the gun to the old man.

"Last one," he said with a shrug, even though he didn't have to.

They both knew the stakes now.

He reloaded the gun and handed it back to her.

"We need to draw it in close," she said, looking directly at the old man.

"I guess by '*we*' you mean me," the old man responded. He shrugged and started to inch towards the edge of the roof, closer to where the lioness waited. "Just be ready." He said to her.

The old man, holding on to a corner, hung his legs over the edge of the roof. He scissored them and kicked the wall, all while screaming at the lioness. "Come and get it you mangy tomcat! Fresh man legs! Come on bitch!"

Janet rolled to her stomach, braced herself, and looked down the barrel of the dart gun.

The lioness walked closer, her tail flicking and its ears back, as if calculating the distance to the old man's dangling legs.

KJ lay prone with the gun over the edge, pointed down at the cat.

One shot.

The lioness put her front paws up on the wall and stretched her muzzle up towards them, peeling back its lips to reveal great yellow fangs that had torn plenty of flesh. The big cat was close.

KJ squeezed. The dart buried itself into the lioness's flank.

The big cat jumped. She ran a quick circle in the dirt, biting at the site of the intrusion.

KJ grabbed the back of the old man's shirt and pulled him back up onto the roof. They collapsed in a heap, breathing hard and letting the tension flow out of them.

"Nice shooting Hawkeye." The old man finally said.

"Never in doubt." KJ returned. "What happens now?"

"We wait." He said. "If it's going to work, it will take a few minutes."

Eventually, the big cat started to pant and stumble. Finally, she fell over, tried to get up but then collapsed into a fitful, anesthetic trance.

They kept an eye on her as they climbed back down from the roof and into the office. The lioness lay panting on its side. She still struggled to get up, but she couldn't.

Bill sniffed at her but kept his distance.

The lioness was at their mercy, but they decided to leave her. They couldn't be sure how long the tranquilizer would keep the cat incapacitated.

The old man, Bill, and KJ returned to the farm building to retrieve their gear and do a quick, but rigorous search to make sure they had the drugs they needed.

The old man found a stack of animal chow bags in a closed cabinet that had been protected from predation. It looked and smelled like dog chow. At least a reasonable facsimile of dog chow. He topped off Bill's packs.

They retreated from the park. It had been an unexpected and harrowing adventure, but they did find what they had been looking for.

***

"I hope she's OK," the old man said as he pushed the cart down the gravel road at a brisk pace.

Janet responded, "We should have killed it or tied it up or something. What happens when she wakes up? Are we going to be able to put enough distance between us?"

"We'll be fine. Lions aren't vindictive. She won't range that far, and Bill will let us know if there's a threat."

"OK Gramps, but if the lioness shows up, I'm letting her eat you next time," she said, adjusting her long frame in the cart.

Bill trotted along at the front as always, on duty as a canine picket.

The old man brightened. "I think we got off fairly well in this adventure. We got some antibiotics for your foot, we didn't get eaten, *and* the day's not even over. Look on the bright side!" He winked at the back of her head and gave the cart a big shove.

Janet gripped the bucket sides. "The bright side?" She asked, "The world sucks now. Everyone I loved is gone and this world keeps trying to kill me every damn day." She turned her head to look at the old man. "Where exactly is '*the bright side'* in all this?"

"We're still alive." The old man replied. "And we're not alone..." he added hesitantly, as if saying this was somehow admitting to a weakness.

"You know I thought about feeding you to that lioness back there so I could get away?" Janet said, half apology, half fact.

"But you didn't." The old man concluded. The conversation ended in the somber, pregnant silence of the unsaid.

The cart creaked. The rickety wheels clattered and kicked up gravel.

The sun was setting low behind the kudzu-covered trees. It glinted off the river and highlighted the cloud of dust trailing this unlikely tribe.

Each day was equal parts puzzle, challenge, and gift after the apocalypse.

Chapter Twenty-One – On the Road

February 1st – Twelve weeks since the virus ended the world…

Janet was roused from her sleep by the cry of a bird in the waking dawn.

She momentarily tensed while orienting herself.

With each day of travel, they slept somewhere new. She tried to remember where they were now.

Her situation – where she was and who she was – slowly crystallized and she relaxed slightly.

This mental recalibration was followed by familiar emotional waves. A wave of sadness ragged with anger swept over her as other memories of what she had been and what she had lost began their daily parade.

Janet pulled an arm from the sleeping bag, rubbed her eyes, and smoothed back her hair, scratching under the worn beanie hat she slept in.

There had been a time when she did not need to start the day by remembering where she was and how she got there. Lying here, in this half-built home, she wondered how her life could have possibly changed so much, and how she was supposed to keep on living.

She was starting to lose touch with the old life, before the world ended. The reality of the previous version seemed less tangible. More like someone else's life. Like scenes from a movie she had watched.

In this half-remembered movie of her old life, the main character woke blurry-eyed to an alarm clock blasting the first few bars of Axle Rose screaming 'Welcome to the Jungle' from her playlist. The song, twenty years past its release date at the time but still as meaningful to her and energizing as it had been in college.

In the scene, she rolled away from the warm embrace of her husband and into her workout clothes to enter the frothing river of another day.

Her city life had been one long frenetic list of urgent appointments. Tooth and nail. A running skirmish with the advancing picket line of obligations. She had jumped into the daily storm of work with her girdle of commitment, a shield of energy, and a sword of intellect held high.

In this full regalia, she would slash a daily path forward in her career only to shed her armor and return home for a hug, a late dinner, and to tuck her kids into bed.

It had been an exhausting life. But it had been her life: Her real life. In that world, she never had to figure out where she was when she woke up.

At that time, outsiders might say her life was hard. But to her it was purposeful and that, in its way, was comforting.

Now, in this new version of her life, every day was a dark mélange of survival. Her list of appointments was condensed to *survive* and *keep moving* and she was not sure she would ever regain her previous sense of purpose.

Maybe it was some version of shock from the abrupt change. Maybe she would eventually make a full transition from the past into the now. But, until that time, every morning she had to remember where she was, who she was with, and suffer through the stroboscopic illusion of the memories of what she had lost.

The last vestiges of sleep cleared, and the echoes of her old life fell away and she remembered fully where they were. They were camping at an abandoned construction site. The bones of a new house being built for the ever-expanding, rapacious, slash-and-burn march of the human race.

There was the smell of lumber and dust. A cool wind bothered the edges of a plastic tarp that flapped sullenly against the unfinished roof above.

She looked down to where the old man lay in his bag, eyes closed, mouth open. If not for the slight snoring and nearly imperceptible movement of his ragged mustache, he looked like yet another corpse.

The big dog lay beside the old man, close enough so there was no way the old man could move or leave without the dog being roused as well. The pooch was lying on its side, paws twitching occasionally.

They were safe for now. Traveling west with the old man was starting to feel like a routine of its own.

Janet rolled back and stared up at the unfinished rafters in the predawn moonlight. She felt the scrape on her elbow and the bruise on her hip. She smiled, despite her tiredness and rubbed sleep from her eyes. Yesterday had been an interesting day.

Since their adventure with the lion, they had been moving north away from Georgia into the Eastern Tennessee foothills, roughly following back roads and dirt paths, keeping the river to their left.

They had been avoiding towns and humans. The old man seemed more comfortable on the lesser-traveled roads. She supposed he had been a loner in his previous life.

To think that just a little more than a few weeks ago, when she encountered him at the dig site, she had been weighing whether he was a threat. She had been open to, even contemplating, that she might need to end his life to save her own. But she had let him minister to her infected foot and she had begun to travel with them.

Things were different now. She now felt an odd tribal fraternity to this old man and dog that she would not have wanted anything to do with in her previous life. She would have walked by them without a second glance in the city, her heels clicking a ferocious pace across the pavement to the office.

Now they were becoming...what? Traveling companions? Like passengers on a train going in the same direction? No, it was more than that. Friends, maybe?

Was her falling in with them just a manifestation of a basic human desire? Was it just human nature? People were inevitably drawn to each other. Especially in times of catastrophe.

The old man and the dog were traveling west. They had a direction and a purpose. And that kept them alive. She could share that purpose in some small way and, just maybe, gain some purpose of her own.

Her foot was better. The old man had, to his credit, helped. It was healed enough to walk on now. The antibiotics from the animal farm had worked wonders.

That was one stark difference. In her old life, an infected toenail wouldn't have threatened her with an early death. Beyond the relief of healing, there was another important thing. She had to trust him, to trust someone else, to set her superhero persona aside and accept help.

And it had worked out.

***

Thank God she was healed and could walk!

She wouldn't be getting back into that cart contraption that the old man had slapped together back at the dig site. She wouldn't be pushed by the old man anymore. Especially after yesterday's debacle.

She remembered it like a slapstick comedy, even though she could have been killed. That would have been ironic, to survive the plague and die by accident on the road.

It started with the hills.

As they traveled further west, the hills became bigger. Rolling wrinkles in the Appalachian landscape. The old man was clearly struggling to push her in the cart up those hills as they got longer and steeper.

She had offered to get out and walk. He had insisted that she wasn't healed enough and continued to struggle through. She was surprised at his strength and endurance. There was some deep fitness hidden in those old, skinny legs.

For the last couple of days, they had been going very slowly as he was forced to rest more in his efforts.

He was in good humor, though. He seemed to be warming to her company as well. He continually made old man jokes about Hanibal crossing the Alps and Edmund Hillary freezing to death on the slopes of Everest.

And, like Hillary, it was not the uphill that finally tolled the death knell to the rickety conveyance. It was the down.

The cart had no brakes. And, along with the increasing size of the uphill pushes came steeper downhill portions where the old man was forced to battle the momentum of the cart.

He would grip the push-bar and dig in his heels in an effort not to be overwhelmed by the gravity of the hill. But his lack of mechanical assembly skills became evident as, on a particularly aggressive downhill, the wire he had used to attach the bar finally gave out.

She remembered the snap and release of it. She had that image of the old man, dumbfounded, holding the detached bar in his hand, helpless to stop the motion of the cart and rapidly receding as she and the cart broke away then, free of his checking force.

He dropped the bar and sprinted after her, but she was now on an uncontrolled sleigh ride down the hill and was gaining speed. The dog was faster and managed to close the ground between them but was ill-equipped to slow her descent. He barked and bit at the spinning tires to no avail.

All she could do was hold on.

The cart bounced and danced over the rutted road and threatened to overturn. It careened closer to the side, and bushes and tree limbs scraped at her.

She kept her head and leaned her weight away from the trees in a clumsy effort to steer. But she was running out of road.

There was a sharp turn coming and a line of large trees. She couldn't hear the old man shouting over the noise of the dog barking, and gravel shooting up to buffet metallic machine-gun impacts on the bottom of the bucket. The bushes along the roadside were a blur.

Her mind flashed back to pushing her kids around the market aisles on their Saturday shopping trips. How she would give the shopping cart a shove and let them coast a few feet. They would laugh and beg for more.

But this was no shopping cart. It was an amateur construction of bailing wire and miscellaneous parts that the old man had put together so she could keep off her infected foot. And now it was careening out of control and coming apart and the trees were closing fast despite her attempts to redirect its progress.

She had to do something.

She gritted her teeth, reached to the right, and jammed the end of one of her crutches into the spinning spokes. The cart shuddered as the crutch caught and locked the wheel. The cart tried to pull right in a sudden lurch but wasn't going to make it. She felt it leaning and beginning to roll and she would be crushed underneath it.

In the spirit of self-preservation, she kicked free of the cart and launched herself using the momentum as it began to cartwheel out of control.

Janet was airborne.

In the memory of it, she could see snapshots of the cart tumbling and herself flying.

She had managed to tuck herself into a ball and had luckily found a softer spot of sand and gravel to roll into. The cart was not so lucky. It continued to cartwheel into the trees and impacted with a great crunch, sending splintered branches and bits of machinery exploding.

The dog finally caught up and licked at her with concern as she sat in the dirt checking to see what, if anything, was broken.

In the end, she had limped away with some scratches and bruises, but otherwise ambulatory and functional.

The old man ran up next breathing heavily and looking panicked with concern. As much as she assured him that she was ok, he still fretted and pestered her to sit down while he made a rote examination. He checked for broken bones or a concussion, but in the end could find nothing serious.

Janet was struck by how genuinely relieved he was that she was ok.

She had made a joke about his driving skills, and they had laughed.

But they needed to be careful. In the apocalypse, the injuries could pile up and take you out with accumulated attrition and fatigue.

In the end, the 'cart crash calamity', as the old man began referring to it, served to deepen their shared experience and strengthen whatever bond was solidifying between the survivors.

Now, she lay here listening to the wind and birds. The old man slept. She was stiff from the crash and from sleeping outside on the ground.

She could walk now, which meant she could walk away. She didn't need them anymore. She could go off on her own. She was confident that she had what it took to survive in this new life.

At one point, she might have killed him. But, instead, she had been relying on him to stay alive.

Trusting anyone was hard now. It took time and effort to trust.

But he could have left her, too, at any point.

His gruff acceptance and active care for her was a voluntary act of humanity on his part. That made him a decent person. Didn't it?

She drew down the zipper of the sleeping bag and shrugged out of it. The dog had one eye open now and was watching her, drowsily. She grunted as she stood. Her left hip was a bit tight. She stretched and stifled a yawn.

The dog rolled over into a sphinx position and cocked his head questioningly as he looked at her.

"Good morning to you too, Rover."

The big tail thumped the unfinished particleboard floor twice.

The old man roused, pushing up onto an elbow groggily. "What?"

"I said" She began, "Have room service send up cappuccino and baguettes, I've got a craving."

The old man smiled. "Best I can do is a can of sardines."

"Oh, the indignity!" She pretended to be disappointed, her smile giving her away.

"Hey," The old man said, looking around the site, "There's probably material to build another cart here."

"No, no, and a thousand times no!" She laughed. "I'll walk from here, thank you very much. You've been kind enough to help me through, but at this point, I'm safer on my own propulsion than in one of your slipshod contraptions."

"Suit yourself, Missy." The old man feigned offense.

Janet looked at the sun rising through the pine trees and again heard the sharp cry of the bird that had woken her. Some sort of raptor, maybe an eagle. Things with claws and talons still hunted in this new world. They still needed to eat. Life went on.

Her new life went on too. In no small part due to the assistance of this old man and his dog. He seemed gruff and distant most of the time. He was fighting his own demons. But he was real.

He was humanity.

Chapter Twenty-Two - The Gauntlet

"I don't like it," KJ said.

"Of course, you don't," the old man replied. "Besides the obvious answer that the world has gone to hell, why not?"

"There's too much smoke. Why would there be so much smoke this many weeks in? Who's burning stuff and why are they doing it?"

"Maybe it's a barbeque," the old man joked. "Ya know, short ribs, beer... It does smell like cooking meat."

"Maybe they'll barbeque your scrawny ass, old man," she countered. "It smells more like plastic or tires or something."

Bill sniffed at the air and didn't seem pleased with what he smelled, but for now, he could only pace and offer up an occasional worried whine.

"I don't know..." The old man thought aloud. "We need supplies, and let's face it, a lot of stuff burns in the apocalypse. That's just a normal day."

He continued. "There probably used to be thirty or forty thousand souls living here in pre-pandemic times. Now there are probably less than a thousand, max, that's if any of them hung around. A couple of crazies… firebugs maybe… I don't see much of a threat."

She eyed him and said, "It's your funeral, old man."

"Great," he responded. "We'll just sneak in and take a look around. With just the three of us, we can disappear back into the brush if there's trouble…"

"How's the foot?" he asked as an afterthought.

"Serviceable," she answered. "Thanks for asking."

Her toe was still looking ugly. The nail was gone, and an angry bluish-red pit hid the new one starting to grow back. But the swelling and pain was down. She could walk and even run some on it.

It was a good thing too, because they had been forced to abandon the cart. The old man's lack of engineering skills became evident when the thing crashed.

They were perched on a bluff overlooking a small city to the south. Through a mix of smoke and the rising morning mist over the river, they could see the layout of the town.

Older, two-story buildings of Main Street bled out into car dealerships and strip malls that sprawled along the generic two-lane road as it headed west toward the river.

Past this commercial center, on the outskirts of town, the smoke seemed to thicken around what looked to be a ballpark or small stadium of some sort, tucked up against railroad tracks that paralleled the river.

Another cookie-cutter small city in the middle-of-nowhere Tennessee. Another metropolis laid low by the virus as it swept through the heartland.

Most of these cities were abandoned now. They were charnel houses occupied by ghosts.

There would be dead down there.

In front of the courthouse, or the clinic, or in the parking lot of the Piggly Wiggly, they would likely find stacks of the dead, as the virus overwhelmed the locals and they tried to respond or escape, with nowhere to go.

There might be a few shell-shocked survivors hiding in the remains. Living their bleak existence.

The good citizens of whatever this place was called had been culled. Their meat left to rot and their bones thrown on the pile of bones that was civilization's legacy.

***

The dirt road wound down the hill to the edge of town. Bill ran ahead as KJ and the old man jogged slowly and cautiously, kicking up gravel and dust along the shoulder of the steep descent.

As the road leveled out, they found themselves threading their way through well-established and shaded suburbs.

Cement sidewalks that humped up where the roots of old maple trees had applied decades of pressure.

Low-slung and tidy ranch houses with a canopy of trees for shade.

As they jogged through the bedroom community, it could have been any quiet Sunday morning.

But this wasn't the peace of the Day of Rest. This was the silence of death.

"It's pretty... but creepy." The old man spoke in a low voice. "Should we look around in some of the houses?"

KJ looked suspiciously at the houses. "Let's keep moving and see if we can find a store or something. I don't want to tangle with a scared homeowner with a gun. The risk isn't worth the reward."

They began to see more familiar signs of the apocalypse as they continued into the city downtown...if you could call it a city. It was more of a large town.

There was the general sense of untidiness - life interrupted. Some crashed and abandoned cars. Occasional broken windows. Small shreds of evidence of vandalism and looting...

And, of course, the dead.

The old man and KJ had to hold their noses when they passed on the far side of a medical center of sorts, where the peak of this town's tragic story likely played out. The last, dying hopes of the townsfolk were evident here as the entrance was littered with bodies.

Other signs of the town's last days were more subtle.

One man's body, just outside the open front door of a well-manicured home, lay prostrate on the lawn. In a dark green bed of irony, he slowly fed the grass he had so lovingly tended.

The old man wet a bandana from his canteen and pulled it across his face.

They checked some stores for supplies as they progressed, but the pickings were slim. They weren't the first, or probably even the second or third group of survivors to pass through. Most of the food and water was gone.

They grabbed what food they could. These were the items that languished in the back of pantry shelves across America, bought by accident, or for a special dish that was never made and forgotten until they expired, or the house was sold.

The old man considered a can of bean sprouts. "Probably burn more calories opening this than you'd get from eating it." He said.

"Beggars can't be choosers," Janet said, inspecting a can of pumpkin pie mix and stuffing it into her bag.

"Geez..." The old man was reading the torn label on a can of chocolate frosting with sprinkles. "Survive the plague only to die of diabetes..."

They continued their foraging as they went and managed to get a change of clothes and some other handy items. At this point in the apocalypse, it was easier to find new clothes than to bother with cleaning the old.

As they left the town center, heading toward the river, there was more smoke in the air. They were getting closer to the source. It smelled acrid. This wasn't campfire smoke. It smelled more like burning garbage.

"Should we avoid this?" Janet asked.

"There might be a larger survivor community here." The old man said. "Maybe they can tell us about the local situation, and I might learn something that would help to find Paul." He looked pensive at the sound of his son's name.

"We don't know if they will be hostile or friendly." She countered.

"We're here now," he continued, "We might as well see what's going on, I think it's worth the risk if we get more information." He sounded like his mind was made up. "The smoke is coming from over by that ballpark." He pointed with his whiskered chin to the stadium-like structure.

"OK, let's take it slow and careful." She replied tugging the new ball cap she had found tighter onto her head and pushing hair out of her eyes.

They skirted a chain link fence and cautiously entered the large parking lot of the ballpark they had seen from above. The sign said, "Taylor Park, home of the Eustis City Woodpeckers."

The old man chuckled and repeated, "Woodpeckers? That's a great name! I bet they struck terror into opposing teams!" He hadn't noticed that the dog had stopped and was looking at them with alert eyes.

"Shut up!" KJ hissed. "There's something not right here. The dog looks worried. What's with all the trash and damage? Something happened here, and it wasn't a baseball game. Looks recent."

"Maybe they used this place as an emergency medical evacuation site or shelter early on?" The old man suggested, but stopped talking when he got one of her patented evil-eye looks.

The main gate of the park had been set in a red brick facade. But now it was torn out, like some malevolent giant had reached down and yanked it free. The grass and brickwork around the gate were shredded as well. There were deep tire tracks and muddy damage. There was a backhoe off to the side with the remains of the crumpled gate.

"You hear something?" The old man asked.

"Music," KJ confirmed. And it was coming from inside the park. It was some old rock and roll that she vaguely recognized.

"Creedence." The old man said, "Green River." He got another *'shut the fuck up!'* look from KJ. "Curiouser and curiouser!" He whispered.

"Let's get out of here," Janet said. "We've got what we need."

The old man looked at her. "No," he said, "There's someone in there and I'm going in to find out who. You can stay if you want. I'm going in."

The old man retrieved his crossbow from his pack, cocked it, and nodded at Janet. She stared back at him, her brow creased.

"You're a fucking idiot." she finally said in a low voice. "Now I have to go with you to make sure you don't get killed."

She picked up a piece of steel rebar from the remains of the gate. It was mostly straight, about a foot long, and with a nasty, jagged point at the end where it had been wrenched from the foundation. She picked up a bit of plastic from the trash and wrapped this around one side to create a grip.

There might be people who needed help here. There might also be people who needed killing, and she would be ready either way.

"OK," she said, "Let's go before I change my mind."

They made their way towards the gaping maw where the gate had been. They could see the lush green of the playing field at the end of the dark tunnel, like a porthole looking out into another world from the darkness.

Bill paused and sniffed. He looked down the tunnel and then back at them with his 'here we go again' look that he got when clearing buildings.

Then Bill led the way as they slowly edged along the cold concrete walls into the gloom. From the darkness, the sun-drenched field had a bright, welcoming, green glow. If it wasn't for the smoke, you might think it was a good day for a ball game.

The rhythmic strains of Green River faded out and the song Commotion started, but something didn't sound right, like the music was playing at too slow a speed. The off-speed music added to the eerie claustrophobia of the tunnel.

The old man's sandals crunched on broken glass, and he worried about the dog, but Bill knew what he was doing, perhaps better than KJ and the old man.

Ahead, the sun poured warm through the opening to the field, and he felt like running to the light and out of this claustrophobic passage.

But KJ was right.

They needed to go slow.

Something had happened here.

It felt wrong, but they had made it this far and needed to find out.

All three paused at the edge of the opening and let their eyes adjust to the sun.

What came into view was surreal. The bright green of the once immaculate infield was littered with trash. There were cars and trucks strewn about, some still smoldering.

There were pieces of furniture – couches and mattresses – dirty with trash, and arranged around the scar of what must have been a huge bonfire.

KJ suppressed a shiver as she thought back to childhood afternoons with her father at a ballpark, not unlike this one. Popcorn, hot dogs, and pop as they cheered on the local boys of summer.

The contrast here with her happy memories was dramatic...almost evil.

This scene in front of her was more than vandalism.

It was sacrilege.

It was the despoiling of hallowed tradition.

Bill whined low and long, a sad keening as he appraised the scene.

It was a sound of mourning.

"Oh my God!" KJ gasped.

The old man stopped and went to one knee.

There were bodies.

But these weren't the unlucky and hapless dead that the virus left in its wake.

These were desecrations.

These were bodies tied to stakes that had been driven into the base paths.

There were bodies hung from and twisted into the backstop fence like something out of a horror movie.

They were hung like Christ figures from an old church. Their clothes were torn and bloody. Their heads hung on loose shoulders hiding bruised faces.

At least a dozen bodies in all that had been killed here - murdered or ... *sacrificed?*

"What the hell *is* this?" The old man asked through clenched teeth. He had seen death before, he had seen executions and man's casual disregard for human life, but it was never easy, and this was bad.

Here before them was a new level of evil.

"We should get out of here," Janet said in a low voice.

"No, wait a minute." The old man responded. "Listen. I don't hear anyone, do you?"

The music was coming from one of the cars that was sitting with its door open.

"A cassette tape." The old man whispered, "And the car battery is dying."

Janet cocked her head, and they listened for a long moment. There were no voices or other noises besides the dying cassette that would indicate the presence of humans. There was only the smoke and the smell of death.

After a long minute of silence, Janet looked over her shoulder down the tunnel from which they had emerged and subvocalized, *"I still think we should get out of here."*

The old man shook his head. "To leave this without understanding what happened is more of a risk. No one is here. Let's go investigate."

The tribe of three cautiously picked their way through the broken and empty bottles and trash, trying to piece together the scene. The eerie music from the open car slowed to an unintelligible crawl and then stopped altogether.

"The fire's still smoking," the old man observed. "Whoever did this hasn't been gone more than a couple hours. Keep your head up."

"What a mess..." Janet added choking down the bile that was stuck in her gorge from the smell and sight of death. She had seen so much death from the plague, but this was something new and different – death from violence. That made it more real and made her feel sick. "How many do you think were here?"

"I dunno…to do that much damage I'd guess at least fifty, maybe a hundred? Maybe more?" The old man speculated. "I *do* know that we don't want to meet them."

Amongst the trash and bottles was baseball equipment – gloves, bats, balls – spread around the field.

They approached the area of home plate, where a particular victim had been staked. It might have been a man...what was left of a man.

It was obvious that he had been used as a target for batting practice.

The body was limp, bruised, and battered. The old man resisted an urge to reach down and feel for a pulse. It would be pointless.

"He's gone," he said, looking up at KJ.

"Probably better for him," she said flatly.

The old man leaned in to look more closely.

"Looks like they finished them with a bullet when they were done with whatever sick game this was," the old man continued, looking around the tableau of chaos and horror that the ballpark had become.

KJ repressed an urge to gag. "What a shit show. Why? Why *do* this?"

"When civilization is gone, humans revert to gangs and tribes…" The old man started before realizing that KJ had not wanted an answer.

As he scanned the scene, the old man thought back to the mythology of the mortal 'games' of the ancient Aztecs. Stadiums where the vanquished did not walk away from the contest and everyone knew that the Roman Colosseum was a place of torture and death.

What is it about humans, homo sapiens, that motivates such brutal entertainment?

Tribalism.

The age-old delineation of the world into 'One of Us,' and 'the Others.'

'The Others' were always dehumanized to justify *inhuman* acts.

Centuries of border wars and religious conflict could be summarized as "You are one of us, or you are not worthy of living."

How many steps was it from sports rivalry and hooliganism to the Romans purging Carthage?

Here before them was the awful proof that there was no distance at all between civilization and genocide.

They were startled by a noise from somewhere around second base.

One of the bodies that had been stretched out on the hood of a truck rolled off into the grass with a groan and a thump.

"Bill! ... Guard!" The old man motioned to the body that was now on its hands and knees retching loudly into the grass.

Bill responded, quickly advancing to guard over the intruder.

He growled a low warning at the man, who had now rolled into a slump with his back against the wheel of the truck, eyes closed, shoulders heaving.

KJ and the old man looked at each other, simultaneously acknowledging Bill's dislike, and advancing with caution.

They were standing over the man. Looking down at him. He was greasy and pale. Dirty hair stuck out from under a baseball cap worn backward. He wore a dirty vest over a work shirt and filthy jeans with work boots.

"Hey!" KJ said, sharply.

"You OK, mister?" The old man followed.

The man groaned as he squinted open his bloodshot eyes. "Where is everybody?"

"Who's 'everybody', mister? What happened here?" The old man asked.

A look of comprehension seemed to cross the man's face and mixed into suspicion. "What? Who are you?" His tone changed from confused to guarded.

"I asked first," the old man countered, and gestured to Bill who was acting like he really didn't like this guy.

The man sat up straighter against the truck.

Bill growled aggressively and looked at the old man as if asking, no, *pleading* for permission to tear this man apart.

"I don't think Bill here likes you, mister," the old man continued, "and as long as I've known him, he's been a pretty good judge of character." He paused, took a deep breath, and repeated slowly, "What happened here?"

"I think I must've gotten some bad hooch," the stranger said, shaking his head a bit, although it was obvious that pained him. "Can't trust anything anymore."

"Get up," KJ said.

The man stood with shaky effort and leaned against the hood of the truck. "I don't want no trouble. Just give me a couple minutes to get right and I'll move on."

"Who did this?" KJ asked directly.

The man looked at his shoes and stammered, "I dunno, I wasn't here, I just came in after looking for supplies and must've drank something bad."

"That's bullshit," KJ stated, causing the old man to raise an eyebrow at her. "You're lying," she went on, "What happened here? Who did this?" She lifted the length of rebar and pointed it at the man's Adam's apple.

The man spread his hands in submission and answered. "OK, OK, it was the King."

The old man repeated it in surprise, "*The King*?"

"Yeah, he calls himself 'the King'. He's got a group of hard cases with him that he calls 'the Volunteer Army of Lost Souls' or some shit."

The old man stood with his mouth open, trying to wrap his head around this information.

"What...happened...here?" KJ stared at the man with a look that was cold, hard, and unflinching.

"We, I mean, they... they had a party."

KJ gestured at the staked bodies. "What *happened* here?"

The man smiled weakly. "Some of the locals didn't see eye to eye with the King."

"Jesus..." the old man sighed.

"More like the devil," KJ replied.

They looked at each other for a long moment. The silence was broken by the man.

"Hey, I gotta piss...do you mind?" said the man.

"Go ahead," KJ said, not moving.

The man shrugged his rumpled shoulders and turned away from them to urinate towards the back of the truck.

KJ and the old man conferred in low voices.

"This is some bad work here," he said.

"These are bad people. Dangerous people." KJ agreed.

"This is some medieval crap. What do you think we should do?" He added.

"We should try not to get killed by them."

"Agreed." The old man replied.

While they were conferencing, the dirty man lurched to his knees, one hand braced against the truck's side, and began heaving again.

"The wages of sin..." the old man said to KJ and shaking his head moved forward to help the man up. "Let's go, partner..." The old man reached to grab the dirty man's shoulder.

But the man turned quickly and spun to grab the old man in a choke hold from behind, brandishing a hunting knife towards KJ.

KJ tensed, surprised.

Bill growled, ears back, hackles raised.

"Get out of my way and no one gets hurt!" He snarled. "I'm gonna get out of here and catch up with the King."

He was sliding along the length of the truck in the direction of the gate, moving the old man along with him as a shield.

Bill held his ground, teeth bared, growling.

"Call off the dog or I'll kill you!" The man threatened, waving the knife.

"I don't think so..." The old man felt his anger rising and came to a decision. "Bill! Faas!"

The old man dropped his weight and tried to swing an elbow into the dirty man's ribcage.

Before anyone even sensed movement, the big dog was airborne. The dog moved so fast that the man had no chance to use the blade. Bill clamped his jaws down on the man's wrist and started viciously jerking back and forth.

The dog's muscles twitched in the effort, standing out like taut ropes along his neck and back.

The man screamed and struggled. He viciously grabbed hold of the old man's hair. "*Get it off me*!"

KJ moved almost as quickly as Bill had. She slipped in with cold, deliberate, and deadly ease, like a ballet dancer or a fencing instructor.

With a violent lunge, she drove the improvised rebar weapon deep into the man's neck.

He dropped the knife and released his grip on the old man, who wriggled free with a shove.

The dirty man fell to his side in the grass, clutching at his neck. Blood gurgled from his mouth. He clawed frantically at the rebar, his eyes wide with desperation and fear as he stared at KJ.

"You can keep that, asshole," KJ said with an emotionless finality.

The old man looked at KJ with surprise. He recovered his composure and told Bill to stand down. He then leaned over to examine the struggling man in the grass.

"Looks like you caught one of the carotid arteries," the old man noted in his professional doctor's voice and turned to look at KJ. "I don't think there is any hope to save him."

"That's probably for the best," she shrugged. "I think saving him would be doing the world a disservice."

The man's struggles were over in a couple of minutes as he bled out into the grass next to the truck, the deep red blood turning black in the brilliant green grass of the infield.

"What do we do now?" The old man asked. He was a little bit surprised at how little emotion KJ seemed to be showing.

His mind drifted.

And he thought again about dehumanization.

And he thought again of the looming specter of the great pile of bones.

And he wondered *again* about his own sanity and what *he* was still doing in this world...

Until KJ's response broke his trance.

"I think we get out of here, collect what we need, and get back into cover," she answered, and she turned to make her way toward the tunnel. "Who knows when the King and his army of assholes might turn up again."

"Do you think anyone is going to miss that guy, back there, and maybe come looking for him?" The old man asked.

"I don't think so." KJ thought about it. "With everything that's going on, no one will miss one random dirtbag. They'll just assume he wandered off. If they do find him, they'll think the locals found him. Didn't he say there were others living here?"

"I suppose you're right, but now we know there are other survivors and some of them are violent and dangerous and, at least semi-organized." The old man said, looking around.

"We need to get out of here," KJ said. "Quickly and quietly. While we still can."

"No argument here," the old man agreed as he followed, shaking his head and taking one last distasteful look around the ballpark.

Chapter Twenty-Three - The Road Ahead

February 7th – Thirteen weeks since the virus ended the world…

"Ear wax," the old man said.

"Here we go again..." Janet rolled her eyes and lay back against the rock outcrop, using her pack as a rough pillow. She arched her back like a cat, stretched her arms out over her head, and relaxed to look at him.

"No, seriously," the old man continued, "How do you deal with ear wax in the apocalypse? You can't see into your own ears…"

"I'm *not* touching your disgusting old ears," Janet responded, hoping this was the end of this particular conversation.

They were on a bluff a couple hundred feet above the river. She looked down and across the muddy flow at the smoke rising from the small city that squatted just above a narrow set of rapids in the river.

There was a bridge spanning the watercourse. It was dotted with abandoned cars and trucks. Large pieces of wrecked junk tangled with uprooted trees and branches were pressed against the up-river side of the bridge. A sipping container was sticking half out of the water, near one shore, jammed against a support pylon.

Bill the Dog had found a high spot a few feet away. He was relaxing in the morning sun and keeping watch at the same time. He rose up onto his haunches and stiffened as a couple of red squirrels chittered around one of the lodge pole pines.

"Leave it, Bill," the old man instructed without much force. Bill relaxed and went into his own 'downward dog' stretching routine that ended with a tremendous dog-yawn.

Janet looked up and gestured to the city. "Do you think the Army of Assholes is over there?"

The old man thought about the question, frowned, and squinted into the southern sun. "Dunno, maybe. Sure seems to be a lot of destruction."

She sensed he was on the verge of yet another monologue on ear wax or ancient Carthage or something equally pedantic and changed the subject with a question.

"What's your story?" She asked and realized it sounded abrupt, maybe even lawyer-like, so she softened the question by adding, "I mean we've been traveling together for a few weeks now and I really don't know your story. Where were you when it happened?" She didn't need to state what *it* was. "Seems like you were already retired? Hiking in the woods or something?"

She studied him closely to gauge his body language.

It wasn't what she expected.

The old man snorted. "Hah! You sound like a lawyer! Should I have my attorney present for this cross-examination?"

She could see that he wasn't angry, more like amused. But why the evasion? Had he been someone famous? She thought he looked familiar. Why was he being evasive, even if it was in this convivial way?

She couldn't help herself. She wanted to know more about him. She kept her eyes locked in, to see if he was hiding something. She ignored his question and continued in the same vein.

"I mean, you're a doctor. Why weren't you working emergency response in a hospital in the city or something? Wasn't it *all hands on deck*?"

"True," he replied, more somber now. "To answer your pointed question, no, I wasn't *hiding* from the medical response... Just the opposite. In fact...in yet another proof of God's sense of humor, they threw me out years ago."

"Why?" Janet asked like the lawyer she was, still watching him.

"It's a long story." He waved his hand dismissively and paused, "It doesn't matter now."

She pressed. "What happened? If it doesn't matter now then you can tell me..." She let the silence lie there like a black hole.

He looked at her and shrugged. "I let my ego get me caught up in a shady business deal. In my defense, I really had nothing to do with the scheme, but I was on the board, so I got caught up in the blame wave." He had an unfocused and faraway look, like he was trying to remember something from long ago.

"I got fired and lost my license," he went on. "Then my wife left me and took the kids and the house." He paused. "I lost everything... I ended up leaving the country for a couple of years. I worked in Africa where they weren't so concerned about the details of my separation from the medical community."

Again, he paused and looked at her. "In hindsight, it's funny. I lost my career and my family, but I learned to live again. I lost everything, but in a way, I found myself."

He let that sink in, then continued.

"Then I found trail running. I found it was something that quieted the demons in my mind. It gave me something to do, kept me from thinking too much, and gave me a new circle of friends who didn't care... hell, they didn't even ask... about my *past*."

He rubbed his eyes and looked up at her with a grin. "In a way, I've been running for years. Even before this shit show began. And *that* is where I was when the virus hit. Out in the woods running the trails with my buddies."

KJ stared at the river below. She thought she could see ripples on the surface. It looked like when fish surface to take a fly, the flick of a dorsal fin sends little waves out in a circle.

She made a mental note. *There is still life out there*. Fish were still going about their fish days, unconcerned with the fate of humanity.

She, returned her gaze to the old man and asked, gentler this time, "Which company? What was the company you were on the board of?"

"Oh, it wouldn't matter to you. It wasn't a well-known company, more of a startup," he said.

"Don't be too sure. You know I was an attorney, but I don't believe you know that the focus of my practice was helping the victims of medical malpractice."

"It was a birth control device maker," he explained. "Medagentix."

He paused long and thought back, sifting through memories that once haunted him. "Apparently, they were falsifying clinical data. I was narcissistic enough to think they were paying me for being a great doctor. But they were paying just to be *associated* with me. Turns out I was just part of the smoke screen."

There was an extended silence.

Janet thought hard about what she was going to say next.

"It was me," was what she decided to lead with.

"What?" The old man asked.

"I was the lawyer who got your license revoked. They wanted to settle, which may have saved your license, but I wouldn't let them."

The old man was silent. Janet continued.

"That was not a victimless crime," she said. "They were killing women. There had to be consequences. I stood up for those women. You were the collateral damage." She looked at him with hard eyes. "I'd do it again."

The old man looked down at his hands and remained silent. Janet could see his face tense. Wrinkles tightened around his eyes. His brow furrowed. There was a hint of pain there too. She wasn't sure what to say next.

She continued, "Look, I'm not sorry I stopped those men. They were killing women. And you were part of that. Ignorance is not innocence. Companies and people need to be held accountable. That's how the world is kept safe for people to live their lives."

"Fat lot of good it did." The old man bristled. "What about all the people I could have saved if I continued working? How does removing a valuable practitioner from the system help them?"

"That's the way consequences work," Janet responded. "Those people you didn't serve are the consequence of your actions as well."

A long silence fell over the two survivors.

Bill the Dog lifted his head and looked at them intently, trying to decipher this mood change. The piercing cry of a circling raptor tore the silence. Bill looked up at it.

Finally, the old man sighed and dropped his head. "Thank you," he said softly. "You didn't have to tell me. So, thank you."

He took a deep breath, blew it out long and slow, and continued. "At one point in my life, I would have been terribly angry with you. I'm not sure I could have described that fury. But not now. It was hard at first, but in the end, I think it was meant to be. I think it taught me things I needed to learn about myself."

"I got to go to Africa and help people who really needed it. I discovered my love for the outdoors, for trails...and for running. So...yeah...Thank you."

She didn't say anything. She gave him the gift of silence to speak into and he continued,

"Looking back, other than causing a schism with my family, I think it was probably a blessing."

Janet bristled. She was going to have a hard time forgiving this man. Even if it was simply inaction on his part – women died. "I'm glad it all worked out for you," she said sarcastically with acid in her voice. "It didn't work out so well for those women."

The old man had a shocked look on his face. "Look...I...I...I'm sorry," was all he could manage.

"So are the families of those women."

They sat in a cold, hard silence for a long time.

Finally, the old man spoke. "It was only with time that I could wrap my head around what had happened. I came close to ending it all many times. I was sick with despair. Not just for myself and what I'd lost, but for those women and the harm that was done. I deserved to have my license taken. I violated my oath. I did harm."

"But with time I learned to live again. To live with that. Maybe to forgive myself a little bit. To live so that I could help people, maybe balance the ledger if I could. I'm not looking to be forgiven. It can't be undone. I'm just looking for a reason to keep living and survive."

Janet thought about this. This man was an example of the type she spent a lifetime fighting. But now, here, with everyone dead, did it really matter? Was it worth holding a grudge? It seemed to her that she could afford to show some empathy now. The stakes were different.

Janet said carefully, "What happened to your family? When the plague hit?"

The old man's face darkened. "My ex-wife and oldest kid died in the city when it started. I tried to get to them, but the streets were chaos. Before the networks crashed, I got a call from one of my old neighbors. They were gone in the first couple of days when it swept through."

He looked up and across the river to the city where ribbons of dark smoke still rose and drifted sideways on the breeze. "My youngest, Paul, was out here somewhere. He was in and out of college – a bit of a full-time student."

He paused and his face became harder with a look of certainty and commitment. "That's where I'm going. I'm trying to find him," he muttered in a shaky voice. "To close that final open loop. Then I'm going to lay down and give my old bones up to this damned earth." He wiped his hands on his pant legs and stood up.

He turned toward her with a tired emptiness and asked, "That's it. That's my story. I'm trying to survive. To do what good I can do with the time I have left and to find my boy. What about you?"

Janet frowned and gazed with empty eyes at the horizon. "My family, everyone I loved are all dead. I watched my husband, my kids, and my parents die."

"I'm sorry," the old man said.

"But you know what?" Janet asked, then answered her own question, "Now that I'm here, I'm still doing what I do. I spent a lifetime standing up for people, stopping bullies from doing bad things, and making bad guys pay."

She looked at him and spread her hands as if embracing the thought.

"I've always considered myself 'the enforcer' of consequences. I think I'm needed here...now...for what I can do."

"The *Avenging Angel,*" the old man said, the corner of his mouth twitching upwards ironically. "Won't you be needing a mask? And a cape? Maybe a magic sword of some sort?"

"Shut *up*," Janet said, not un-playfully. "I'm serious. I didn't ask for it. I'd rather have my family back, but the universe dropped me here into this pile of shit with a certain set of skills. Maybe I was put here for a purpose?"

"I don't want to be unkind," he responded. "But that sounds a bit self-serving and messianic."

"No more self-serving than you are, you nihilistic old man. You and your pile of bones. You've got a set of skills, too. You may have something to contribute."

"I suppose you're right. It's a clean slate, a level playing field. We're making up our own rules now. Much of what we believed to be true or false...good or bad...is meaningless. Or at least, in flux."

"I'll help you find your son," Janet said softly but decisively, looking at the ground between her feet. "But first, we're going to find this '*King*' and see if we can't stop him. This is something we can do that will save lives and help people – *balance the ledger* as you said." She paused. "How about it?"

The old man considered.

"I would be grateful for your help," he finally responded. It came out more official sounding than he had intended, like some sort of pact or agreement. So, he continued to talk.

"I'm tired," he said, "And I've lived a long life. I'm not sure what the point of surviving is. I mean, really, what's the point? I feel like there's not much keeping me in this world."

Janet looked at him. "So, you're Hamlet now? You're trying to decide if you want *to suffer the slings and arrows of outrageous fortune?* This isn't poetry. We're all tired. It's the apocalypse. We're tired, we're dirty and we're all walking the tightrope between sanity and insanity without a net." She turned her attention to the burning city and continued, "But this is bigger than us. There's an opportunity here. We can make a difference. We can be agents of good against this shitty tsunami of evil."

"OK, Judge Dread," The old man said, "I'll help you go after this King, and you help me find Paul." He continued, "I don't know what we're going to accomplish; one old man, an avenging angel, and a dog, but like I said, I have nothing better to do and it seems like, if we don't get killed, we'll be moving the needle in the right direction."

"It's a deal then," Janet said. She stuck out a hand to shake it. He smiled and grasped.

She felt in her gut she could trust this man, despite his history. There was something there. This might be the purpose she needed to keep going. And she knew, more than anything else, purpose kept people alive.

The old man looked at the ground, moving the dirt about with one foot, and started again, as if he were telling a story. "The last time I saw Paul was a couple of months ago. We hadn't talked for years. My family broke off contact when I lost my license. I was a pariah, and they moved on without me.

"Then, less than six months ago, out of the blue, Paul reached out to me and wanted to meet, to talk. I traveled down to Tennessee, where he goes...went to school, and met with him. When I walked into that coffee shop, he was so different from the kid I remembered. He had grown into such a man. So smart and confident, but at the same time I could sense that he was scared to see me...and angry...still full of anger. It wasn't an easy conversation. There were hard words. There were tears. It ended with shouting and we both said some regrettable things."

The old man's voice broke just a little, then he caught himself, cleared his throat, and continued, "He said he didn't need a father...didn't want a father...He stormed out. There's a lifetime of unfinished business there. I'd really like a chance to make it right...If he'd let me. If he's still alive. If he's out there."

The old man's voice trailed off.

His words hung for a moment in the sounds of birds and of the wind blowing through the dry branches above.

Janet broke the mood, like the popping of pine pitch in a campfire. "OK!" she said brightly and sat up, "Then we'll just have to go find him, this smart young man of yours. We'll find him and invite him to join our team. He'll help us turn the tide. But first, we need to see about this King, take him down a few pegs!"

"When did you get such a positive attitude?" The old man asked. "I just saw you shish kabob a dude with a hunk of rebar. Now you're some self-styled Wonder Woman who's going to fight bad guys and help me find my son?"

He looked down and watched a flock of plovers dip in a synchronous dive across the river, "But I'll take you up on your offer. It's not going to be easy. We're going to have to get across the river. I'm not sure we should use the roads or the bridges. That's a natural choke point for anyone who wants to control the movement of survivors."

"Good place for a trap." Janet agreed.

"Potentially," the old man confirmed. "The King and his army aren't going to be a one-off phenomenon. There will be scared, half-mad survivors clinging to any narcissistic tyrant who thinks he is a new kingdom god."

"Then how come *you* don't have a following?" Janet said wryly.

The old man laughed, "I do. I've got a dog and a psychotic, cut-throat lawyer! My point is, we are going to come across people and situations that are the true manifestations of your *tsunami of crap*."

"Shitty tsunami of *evil*," she corrected him.

"Sure, whatever. I'm just saying, you'd better be willing to strap yourself in because the ride is about to get bumpy."

"Can't be worse than that cart you pushed me in!"

"That bumpy ride was a metaphor. Don't they have metaphors in your superhero world?" He asked.

She held up a hand, "I know what you mean. I know we're in a pile of crap here, but I'm all in."

"What do you plan to do when we find this King?" The old man asked.

"First thing we need to do is find out what's going on – assess the situation. Maybe we can save some people by getting them out of his way. But, make no mistake, if I have an opportunity, I'm more than willing to take him out."

"Judge, jury, and executioner?" The old man asked.

"If it's necessary to save people's lives, yes."

Janet became serious and spoke from her heart, "Look, you and me, even Bill, we're already dead. We're just dust in the wind. Today is all we've got. Let's not worry about what's going to happen next week. Let's go forth and do what we can. If we can do something that's going to help the greater good, let's not think too much, let's do it."

He looked at her, a bit surprised, but nodded his head in sullen agreement, "OK. We'll take it as it comes."

A pair of eagles rode the thermals over the river.

Their wings twitched in the air currents as they subtly maintained their direction and altitude.

They weren't fighting the air, they were riding it, accepting it.

The old man breathed in and lowered his gaze slowly to the river.

Brown smoke curled up towards them from a structure on the opposite bank.

There were bodies on the flat of the bridge nearest to them, dark stains spreading outward as they melted into the dust of the bridge road.

Beyond the bridge, beyond the smoldering city, out there, was the *unknown*.

Out there was more *death*.

More *insanity*.

More *bad men*.

More *evil*.

The *King* was out there.

And *Paul*. Paul was out there.

The old man could feel that now with an undeniable, paternal certainty.

Paul was out there and he...no*, they*—together, they would find him.

Just then a line of vehicles emerged from the smoke, heading towards the bridge.

Janet looked at the old man and said, "Come on, old man, it's time to move!"

Coming Soon

Fear not! The Apocalypse continues!

There are five books in the After the Apocalypse series of which this is the first.

Look for the next installment and keep up to date with everything in our After the Apocalypse community by visiting visit our website at www.oldmanapocalypse.com

Find the Podcast on Acast -> https://shows.acast.com/after-the-apocalypse

Visit the Facebook group -> https://www.facebook.com/groups/oldmanapocalypse

About the Author

Chris Russell is a science fiction devotee who writes from the suburbs of New England. He is particularly passionate about the Apocalyptic genre. He began writing "After the Apocalypse" as an audio podcast in 2020. It has since grown to tens of thousands of monthly listeners across five seasons of the story.

In his spare time, he spends hours running and ruminating in the forest trails with his border collie Ollie.

amcontent.com/pod-product-compliance
Source LLC
N
7111025
0020B/45
7 7 2 3 4 2 0 2 *